THE HIDDEN SHRINE OF TMOCANOTZ

Author: Tom Knauss
Project Managers: Zach Glazar and Tom Knauss
Editor: Jeff Harkness
Art Direction: Casey Christofferson
Layout and Graphic Design: Charles A. Wright
Cover Design: Charles A. Wright
Cover Art: Adrian Landeros
Interior Art: Julio de Carvalho
Cartography: Robert Altbauer

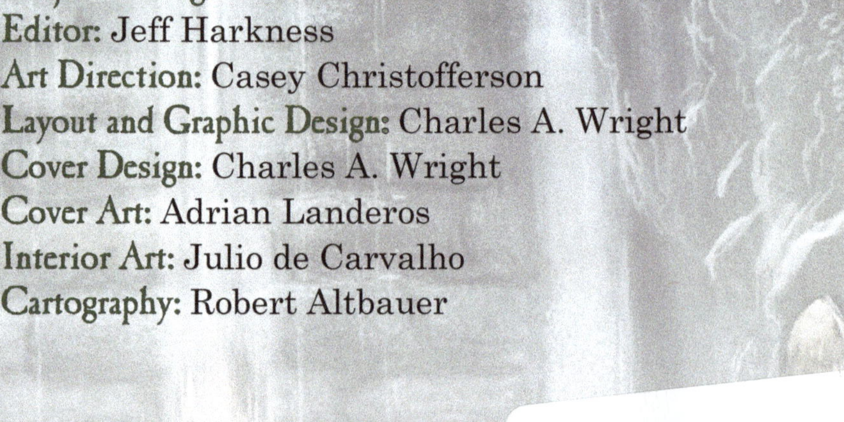

FROG GOD GAMES
ISBN: 978-1-6656-0128-3

FROG GOD GAMES IS:

Bill Webb, Matthew J. Finch, Zach Glazar, Charles A. Wright, Edwin Nagy, Mike Badolato, John Barnhouse

Table of Contents

THE HIDDEN SHRINE OF TMOCANOTZ

"INSANITY HAS NO MASTER."

— AN AZTLI PROVERB

The Hidden Shrine of Tmocanotz is an adventure for four 3rd- to 5th-level characters that introduces them to an old foe making an appearance in the forsaken Izmalli Swamp on the island of Tehuatl. In a subterranean and partially submerged complex beneath the ground, the deranged worshippers of a foul deity have made a sudden and unexpected resurgence in their efforts to spread madness and wickedness beyond their isolated corner of the wetlands.

ADVENTURE BACKGROUND

Long ago, the cipatenhuas migrated to Tehuatl from a distant land. The great sea serpent Cipactli led his minions across Mother Oceanus in their quest to find a new home. When the beast and the crocodilian humanoids under his protection reached the island's shore, their arrival had been expected. The devious god Itztliteotl awaited Cipactli and his followers. The consummate trickster had longed for this opportunity to have some fun at the fearsome yet dimwitted monster's expense, yet in this case, the joke was on him. Unwilling to play the cunning deity's game, Cipactli opened his mighty jaws and clamped down on Itztliteotl's foot, tearing the appendage from the outraged hero-god's leg. In a fit of rage, Itztliteotl slew the mighty beast and hurled his lifeless body back into the sea.

The startled cipatenhuas who followed Cipactli to their new homeland nervously awaited the angry deity's vengeance. But despite their leader's transgression, the Smoking Mirror spared their lives though not without a price. Because they came from the water, he cursed the cipatenhua race, condemning them to never set foot on dry land lest they suffer his wrath. Grateful for his mercy, the reptilian cipatenhuas paradoxically paid homage to the jaguar lord who took pity on their people after exacting his spiteful revenge upon them and their descendants. Confined to the aquatic swamps and marshes along the island's eastern shore, the migrants undertook the arduous task of rebuilding their communities and adapting to a fresh start in a distant land under the aegis of a foreign god and his worshippers, the Aztlis, the island's indigenous humans.

Over the next 1,000 years, the cipatenhuas gradually adjusted to their new lives in Tehuatl. They forged friendly relationships with some of their fellow humanoids while engaging in protracted battles against aggressive adversaries who threatened their territory. Despite their inability to leave the wetlands, many of their race embraced the sly Itztliteotl as their divine benefactor, yet a small minority chafed at the notion of venerating the wily being who condemned them to a miserable existence in the island's stinking wetlands. Unwilling to accept another god indigenous to the island, they turned to a fellow import — the deranged Frog God Tsathogga. Although they expressed some trepidation venerating a deity with no comprehensible agenda other than sowing murder and mayhem, the crazed demon prince seemed to be the best choice in an imperfect world.

One year ago, a small enclave of Tsathogga's cipatenhua worshippers broke away from their community and founded a hidden shrine to their vile god in a catacomb of tunnels and chambers beneath a small pond where they could clandestinely perform their sinister rites. To complete this undertaking, this small band of worshippers led by Griigg the frog prince began kidnapping other humanoids to serve as victims for their sacrificial rites and slaves to perform menial tasks within the shrine. With their power steadily growing, Griigg and his followers now seek to expand their influence and that of their insane benefactor within their isolated section of the Izmalli Swamp.

ADVENTURE SYNOPSIS

The adventure begins with Tsathogga's cipatenhua worshippers venturing outside the secure confines of their underwater complex in a search for fresh victims to sacrifice to their deranged deity or a new batch of slaves to mercilessly toil under their oppressive yoke. The characters may encounter the cipatenhuas during their hunt or they may become embroiled in the adventure's events after being asked to investigate the disappearance of someone who fell prey to the cipatenhuas. The characters may use their tracking ability to retrace the cipatenhuas' steps back to the edge of a pond that houses their subterranean shrine or the characters may discover the shrine's location through other means such as divination spells, information from a cipatenhua still loyal to Itztliteotl, or a captured cipatenhua follower of Tsathogga.

After locating the hidden entrance to the shrine, the characters must access the partially submerged complex through a tunnel filled with murky water. Here, the characters are free to explore the shrine, which includes living quarters for the cipatenhua residents, slave quarters, and food production and distribution areas, and the shrine's inner sanctum. The cunning cipatenhuas incorporated natural and manmade traps into their stronghold to deter intruders and also burrow into the earth searching for precious gemstones. When the characters bypass the shrine's cipatenhua and monstrous guards, they can reach the unholy shrine proper where the characters confront Griigg the frog prince and his demented minions.

STARTING THE ADVENTURE

The characters may start the adventure in one of the Izmalli Swamp's neighboring villages or while traveling to another location within the wetland from somewhere else. If the characters hail from the region, you may have a concerned family member approach the characters and ask them to search for a missing loved one. Alternatively, a religious, political, or economic interest may also solicit assistance from the characters to investigate a disappearance, strange event, or disruption to commercial traffic. For characters also partaking in the adventure *The Re-education of Coyotl*, the town of Teohuacan detailed in that adventure provides a good starting point for the adventurers to begin their quest. Otherwise, you are free to use one of the communities from the *Tehuatl* sourcebook from **Frog God Games** as the characters' home base or you may create another small settlement of your choosing in any setting of your choice. If the characters are not local to the area, they could intervene in the middle of an attempted abduction or fall prey to a cipatenhua ambush while traveling through the area.

ADVENTURE HOOKS

You may use any of the following adventure hooks to immerse the characters into the story or invent one of your own depending upon how and where you want to start the adventure.

ABDUCTION

While traveling through a comparatively dry portion of the Izmalli Swamp, characters have a 2-in-6 chance to hear a commotion coming from the brush ahead. **Three Aztli teenagers** struggle to fend off **6 cipatenhuas** (see **Appendix A: New Monsters**) who accosted them while venturing through the wilderness. The humans appear badly injured, while the cipatenhuas appear virtually unscathed. The humanoids seek to capture rather than kill the adolescents to use them as sacrifices to their profane deity Tsathogga. Alternatively, you may forego the adolescents altogether and instead have the cipatenhuas attempt to ambush the characters. If the characters fail to notice the crocodilian humanoids hiding in the vegetation, the monsters surprise them. Adventurers who defeat the monsters may intensely question them to learn of their intentions, the location of their shrine, and their allegiance to the Frog God Tsathogga. Otherwise, the characters have a 60% chance to retrace their steps back to their shrine (90% for rangers). The trail crosses 1d4 streams along the way, requiring a new check each time.

Aztli Teens (3): HD 1d6hp; HP 5 each (currently 2); AC 9[10]; **Atk** spear (1d6); **Move** 12; **Save** 18; **AL** N; **CL/XP** B/10; **Special:** none. (*Monstrosities* 254)
Equipment: spear.

Cipatenhuas (6): HD 3; HP 22, 19, 18x2, 15, 12; AC 7[12]; **Atk** 2 claws (1d4) or bite (1d6) or club (1d6) and bite (1d6); **Move** 12 (swim 12); **Save** 14; **AL** N; **CL/XP** 3/60; **Special:** camouflage (1-in-6 chance to spot), cursed (must remain on wet land or 1d6 damage every 10 minutes). (see **Appendix A: New Monsters**)
Equipment: club.

Big Fish

Two days ago, Tlacamichi, a local fisherman, told his wife and children that he was going into the swamp to his secret fishing hole and would be home before dusk that evening for dinner. He never came back. Naturally, his wife **Tecaltin** fears for her husband's safety. She swears he would never abandon his family and has tirelessly prayed to Atoyatl to protect him. The distraught spouse implores the characters to find her husband and discover the truth about what happened to him. Tecaltin can provide no specifics regarding the secret fishing hole's precise spot, but believes she knows its general vicinity. She says he primarily caught catfish in what he described as a murky pond a short walk from the riverbank. She cannot pay the character for their services. Instead, Tecaltin frantically begs the adventurers to help her family, who are close friends with some influential people in town.

Tecaltin, Female Aztli Human: HP 8; AC 9[10]; **Atk** dagger; **Move** 12; **Save** 16; **AL** N; **CL/XP** 2/30; **Special:** none. (*Monstrosities* 254)
Equipment: dagger.

Heretics

Itztliteotl's human representative in town, **Huitayo**, greatly fears some of his cipatenhua followers whom he visits from time to time have gone astray from their faith and embraced a heretical new god in a vile shrine hidden somewhere in the wilderness. His most loyal acolyte Tzamma has heard some of his people speak of abandoning the Aztli deity and shifting their devotion to a foul new entity whose followers meet in a subterranean shrine somewhere in the wilderness. Tzamma has no knowledge of the gathering place's exact location, though he believes he knows the general area where it can be found. He agrees to take the characters there to find it and root out the evil within the unholy sanctum.

Huitayo, Male Aztli Human Priest (Clr4): HP 19; AC 6[13]; **Atk** macuahuitl (1d8); **Move** 12; **Save** 12; **AL** L; **CL/XP** 5/240; **Special:** +2 save versus paralyzation and poison, banish undead, spells (2/1).
Spells: 1st—*cure light wounds, protection from evil*; 2nd—*bless*.
Equipment: cipacahuipilli armor[b], macuahuitl[b]
[b] See **Appendix B: New Items and Magic**

Tzamma, Male Cipatenhua: HD 3; HP 17; AC 7[12]; **Atk** 2 claws (1d4) or bite (1d6) or club (1d6) and bite (1d6); **Move** 12 (swim 12); **Save** 14; **AL** N; **CL/XP** 3/60; **Special:** camouflage (1-in-6 chance to spot), cursed (must remain on wet land or 1d6 damage every 10 minutes). (see **Appendix A: New Monsters**)
Equipment: club.

Rumors

Numerous stories of dubious validity circulate among the populace in the region. The characters may overhear these tales being spread in a public setting or learn of them during a conversation with a local inhabitant. Likewise, the characters may have already gained some information about the area and its people through their personal experiences and education. Roll a d20 once on the table below. Give the characters all the information with a target number equal to or lower than the number rolled.

TABLE 1–1: RUMORS

d20	Rumor
1	The cipatenhuas are a race of crocodilian humanoids who arrived in Tehuatl roughly 1,000 years ago. They predominately dwell in the island's marshes and swamps. Although not overly aggressive, the cipatenhuas vigorously defend their territory. (This rumor is true)
2	When the cipatenhuas first arrived in Tehuatl, the Aztli god Itztliteotl cursed them because the giant beast leading them to the island bit off the angry deity's foot. For this reason, the cipatenhuas must always keep at least one foot wet at all times or suffer his wrath. Nonetheless, they primarily worship Itztliteotl though some sects have strayed from the faith over the years. (This rumor is true)
3	The cipatenhuas have an affinity for crocodiles, though some of them can supposedly transform into other reptiles or amphibians. (This rumor is true)
4	Frog people also inhabit the swamp and have been seen in greater numbers over the past several weeks. They seem to be intently searching for something. (This rumor is true)
5	The gnolls from the neighboring grasslands recruited numerous spies throughout the swamp. An invasion may be imminent. (This rumor is false)
6	Someone is raising the dead in the swamp! Bloated, waterlogged corpses are rising from the ground, seeking to feast on the flesh of the living. (Some undead are in the swamp, so this rumor is partly true though no one is actively raising them)
7	If you're inclined to dance, Org, the oafish troll who lives along the river will join you for a song or two. He is friendly with the local teenagers. (This rumor is true)
8	A druid conducts bizarre experiments on the swamp's flora and fauna. Some of his abominations haunt the flooded forest (This rumor is false)
10	A small yet bloodthirsty cult has arisen among the cipatenhuas. They purportedly worship a deity imported from a foreign land. Some even believe they established a shrine within the swamp. (This rumor is true)
11	The cipatenhuas who venerate this god sacrifice living creatures to it. (This rumor is true)
13	A band of warriors swear they saw a small, canine-like humanoid accompanying a cipatenhua in the swamp several days ago. (This rumor is true)
14	Beware the cottage along the river. It is haunted. (This rumor is partially true and refers to Eltezcatl's house, which is dangerous but not haunted)
16	Smugglers transporting illicit goods frequent the river and bury some of their wares beneath the mud for safekeeping. (This rumor is mostly false)
17	The boggards are poised to attack the region. (This rumor is false)

Events

The following vignettes do not play an essential role in the adventure. Instead, they are intended to be interspersed into the story to give the characters additional clues and information in a nonconfrontational setting. You can choose an encounter or roll randomly.

Table 1–2: Adventure Events

d10	Event
1–3	Culalli, Itaca, Nenatl, Yaniyah, Yatzli, and Yotli, six local teenage girls, infectiously giggle while performing a strange dance containing funny movements and silly lyrics. They beg the characters to join them and offer to teach them the odd steps. If the characters refuse to participate, the girls poke fun at them, telling the characters that even the troll by the river has more rhythm and dances alongside them. The girls' reference pertains to the encounter with **Org** detailed in Part One of the adventure.
4–5	Catuma, a local fisherman, has two large catfish in a net slung over his back. He claims the fish are so big that he and his family will be able to eat only one before the other spoils. He offers to sell the other catfish to the characters for the fair price of 2 cacao beans. If asked where he caught the fish, he provides general directions to a pond that is close to Tlacamichi's secret fishing hole from the preceding **Big Fish** adventure hook.
6–7	Two hairless pet dogs stand nose to nose and growl at each other while intently staring at a bone on the ground. The animals trade turns trying to grab the bone before being intimidated out of doing so by their canine counterpart. A character who examines the bone verifies it is not human, though it appears to be part of a flipper from a large aquatic mammal.
8–9	Three teenage boys named Izmalla, Nematzo, and Tetzuo are playing with a ball in an open field. The rambunctious boy converse about an alluring woman they saw walking in the swamp alongside her pet cat. They had never seen her before, but strangely each of their descriptions of the woman are different, yet the cat remains the same. Their discussion centers on the upcoming encounter **The Cat in the Hag's Hat**.
10	Itzlacoytl drank more pulque than humanly possible. He lies on his side snoring loudly as some frothy liquid rolls down the side of his cheek. In his drunken stupor, he periodically blurts out statements about demons coming to get him. If roused from his slumber, the cantankerous old man profusely swears and tells the characters he knows nothing about demons and demands they let him sleep off his dreadful hangover.

Part One: The Izmalli Swamp

Ominous, foreboding, disgusting, sweltering, and sticky are just some of the adjectives people use to describe these wetlands. From an ecological standpoint, the Izmalli Swamp is a semitropical saltwater swamp where roughly half the terrain lies submerged beneath at least several inches of standing water. Ponds, brooks, streams, and small rivers crisscross the soggy landscape with frequent regularity. The stifling heat and humidity wilt even the hardiest creatures within minutes, while iron and steel almost instantly start to rust when exposed to these warm, humid conditions. There are no formal roads or trails anywhere, though the lack of vegetation and slightly drier ground in some areas function as rudimentary paths cutting through the largely untamed wilderness. With the exception of these crude roadways, the balance of the swamp is treated as difficult terrain.

Local inhabitants rarely stray off the beaten path despite the increased likelihood of stumbling into an ambush, a booby trap, or a wild animal making its way through the swamp. Despite the dangers, expeditiousness and the fear of getting hopelessly lost in the uncharted wilderness play an important role in keeping most people from wandering off on their own in the wetlands. For every hour spent trekking through the Izmalli Swamp, there is a 25% chance of encountering one of the creatures appearing on **Table 1–3: Izmalli Swamp Wilderness Random Encounters**. If the characters exclusively remain on the path, the chance increases to 35%, but they encounter only humanoids or monsters. A rendezvous with an animal or monster is rerolled until the adventurers run into a humanoid or monster.

Table 1–3: Izmalli Swamp Wilderness Random Encounters

d8	Encounter
1	1d2 + 1 cipatenhuas plus a cipatenhua disciple
2	1d3 + 3 crocodiles
3	1d2 + 1 giant toads
4	1d3 mudbog oozes
5	2 ogres
6	2 sloth vipers
7	1d4 + 3 tsathars
8	1d3 will-o'-the-wisps

Cipatenhuas

The **1d2 + 1 cipatenhuas** and their **cipatenhua disciple** routinely patrol the area around their shrine as they search for trespassers, fresh prey, and potential slaves. The crocodilian humanoids likely assess the adventurers as falling into the first category if they appear heavily armed and well-equipped. The cipatenhua disciple functions as the group's de facto leader and prefers to use his repertoire of spells to snipe at the characters from afar while the cipatenhuas function as frontline troops. In this endeavor, the disciple may attempt to climb a nearby tree or potentially swim into the middle of a pond or stream and attack from that relatively safe location. Like the cipatenhuas in the preceding **Abduction** adventure hook, the characters can question these creatures to discover the shrine's location or follow their tracks back to the site.

Cipatenhuas (1d2+1): HD 3; **AC** 7[12]; **Atk** 2 claws (1d4) or bite (1d6) or club (1d6) and bite (1d6); **Move** 12 (swim 12); **Save** 14; **AL** N; **CL/XP** 3/60; **Special:** camouflage (1-in-6 chance to spot), cursed (must remain on wet land or 1d6 damage every 10 minutes). (see **Appendix A: New Monsters**)
Equipment: club, 2d6 seashells (1 gp each).
Cipatenhua Disciple of Tsathogga: HD 6; **HP** 40; **AC** 7[12] or 2[17] (missile) and 4[15] (melee) from *shield* spell; **Atk** 2 claws (1d4) or bite (1d6) or club (1d6) and bite (1d6); **Move** 12 (swim 12); **Save** 11; **AL** N; **CL/XP** 6/400; **Special:** camouflage (1-in-6 chance to spot), cursed (must remain on wet land or 1d6 damage every 10 minutes), spell-like ability, spells (4/2/2 MU), touch of madness (1/day, save or babble incoherently for 1d6+2 rounds).
Spell-like ability: 1/day—*polymorph self* (into giant frog)
Spells: 1st—*charm person, jinx*[c], *magic missile, shield*; 2nd—*invisibility, phantasmal force*; 3rd—*instill madness*[c], *hold person*.
Equipment: club, pouch containing six moss agates (10 gp each).
[c] See **Appendix C: New Spells**

Crocodiles

These hungry beasts predominately stick to the waterways and riverbanks in search of prey rather than walk along wet earth or even dry land for their next meal. When the characters encounter the reptiles, they are best suited for a fight in a shallow body of water rather than out in the open. The **1d3 + 3 crocodiles** never fight as a cohesive unit and simply attack the nearest creature with unbridled ferocity. Despite their aggressiveness, the crocodiles are unwilling to risk their lives for a bite to eat. Each crocodile individually retreats back to the water if reduced to fewer than one-half their hit points.

Crocodiles (1d3+3): HD 3; **AC** 4[15]; **Atk** bite (1d6); **Move** 9 (swim 12); **Save** 14; **AL** N; **CL/XP** 3/60; **Special:** none. (*Monstrosities* 77)

TEOHUACAN AND VICINITY
C
Elcomatl River
O
Teohuacan
Lake
Tlacuca
N
Namatl River
1 Square – 1/2 Mile

Giant Toads

Despite the amphibians' affiliation with the vile Frog God, these large beasts are not associated with the shrine in any way. Like the crocodiles, these creatures are best suited for an encounter within or along the edges of a body of water where they can leap onto their prey and bite their opponent. The **1d2 + 1 giant toads** fight as individuals rather than part of a coordinated team.

Giant Toads (1d2+1): HD 3; AC 6[13]; **Atk** bite (1d8); **Move** 6 (hop 30ft); **Save** 14; **AL** N; **CL/XP** 3/60; **Special:** hop (30ft leap). (*Monstrosities* 475)

Mudbog Ooze

Murky pools of water are practically everywhere in the Izmalli Swamp, making it impossible to distinguish these mindless, amorphous blobs of protoplasm from the ordinary muddy pools strewn across the characters' path. Because of their ability to blend into their surroundings, the oozes stretch across the crude trails cut through the vegetation. When a creature steps on one of them or moves within 10 feet, the ooze attempts to engulf its victim and haul it into a neighboring body of water in an attempt to drown it and prevent rescuers from coming to the captured creature's aid. The **1d3 mudbog oozes** have no concept of death so they continue fighting until slain.

Mudbog Oozes (1d3): HD 6; AC 8[11]; **Atk** slam (2d6); **Move** 6 (swim 9); **Save** 11; **AL** N; **CL/XP** 6/400; **Special:** acid (dissolves organic material), camouflage (1-in-6 chance to spot), engulf (after strike, can engulf with next successful strike, 1d6 damage per round, save avoids), immune to blunt weapons. (see **Appendix A: New Monsters**)

Ogres

Tehuatl's small population of ogres generally dwell within the Tepepan Mountains, especially in the town of Hrawrg, otherwise known as Ogretown. However, these **2 ogres** ventured from the comparatively safe confines of their mountainous home into the foul Izmalli Swamp on their way to meet with a fellow giant, Org, the river troll (see the upcoming **Org** encounter for more details) to gather intelligence about humanoid and monstrous activities within the Izmalli Swamp. The ogres, **Grong** and **Hrang**, follow a crude, hand-drawn map detailing how to navigate a path to Org's lair using local landmarks as guides. The oafish brutes cannot willingly pass up on opportunity to attack and bully humanoids smaller than themselves during the course of their mission. Their taste for flesh compels them to mercilessly assault elves, dwarves, and halflings whom they consider a delicacy. Fearful of failing Ogretown's masters, the giants propose a truce with the characters if seriously threatened and offer to take them to Org who may have some knowledge about the cipatenhuas' hidden shrine. If the characters accept the ogres' terms, the giants fulfill their end of the bargain by escorting them to Org's hideaway, though the treacherous ogres once again assault the characters if an opportunity presents itself once they reach their destination. Grong and Hrang know nothing about the Izmalli Swamp outside of their mission to rendezvous with the river troll.

Grong and Hrang, Ogres (2): HD 4+1; AC 5[14]; **Atk** club (1d10+1); **Move** 9; **Save** 13; **AL** C; **CL/XP** 4/120; **Special:** none. (*Monstrosities* 356)
Equipment: club, sack containing 3d6 gp. Grong has a scroll of *bless* he looted from a dwarven cleric he killed in the mountains before the pair began their journey here.

Sloth Vipers

This mated pair of serpents loiters along the banks of a stream, brook, or river where they hid their nest containing three eggs within a dense thicket of vegetation. Characters have a 1-in-6 chance to spot these emerald-colored eggs amid the cluster of twisted vines, leaves, and dirt. Likewise, the ambush predator serpents also conceal their position within the trees. The snakes may either drop down on their intended target and bite it, or snap down on its victim and recoil back up the tree. Driven by instinct, the **2 sloth vipers** never retreat and fight to the death to protect their offspring from falling into humanoid hands.

Sloth Vipers (2): HD 5; AC 6[13]; **Atk** bite (1d4 + poison); **Move** 12 (climb 12, swim 12); **Save** 12; **AL** N; **CL/XP** 6/400; **Special:** poison (save or die). (see **Appendix A: New Monsters**)

Tsathars

The insidious tsathars and cipatenhuas may share the same deity, but their animosity toward each other knows no bounds. The **1d4 + 3 tsathars** believe themselves to be Tsathogga's children, relegating the cipatenhuas to unwelcome stepchildren. The crocodilian humanoids find the monstrous tsathars too deranged for their sensibilities. With this animosity in mind, this large team of tsathars has spent the last several weeks combing the area searching for the hidden shrine to their mad deity. In their warped minds, the cipatenhuas blaspheme their god, which requires them to find the concealed sanctum and corrupt it to their deranged way of thinking. Despite their exhaustive efforts, the entrance to the subterranean complex eludes them at every turn. If the characters encounter the tsathars during daylight hours, the monstrosities exhibit some caution moving about the area. They fan out across a wide perimeter, poking and prodding the ground with their spears in a feeble attempt to find the shrine through tactile examination. When the sun sets, the tsathars display their typical recklessness, blundering across the swamp in a frantic search for a cipatenhua who may lead them to their lair.

Regardless of the lighting conditions, the tsathars primarily rely on their keen sense of smell to detect nearby enemies. When they run across humanoids, the froglike creatures chaotically attack them with unbridled fury, throwing themselves at their foes like a wave crashing upon a beach. Without any leadership, the crazed tsathars attack the nearest creature until they kill it or the tsathar dies in the process of trying. If the characters capture a tsathar and can communicate with it, the prisoner reveals scant bits of information. The tsathar divulges that it hails from the Tlococua Marsh, south of the Great Canal bisecting the island, and that it was sent into the swamp to find the subterranean cipatenhua shrine. Otherwise, the demented tsathar rambles incoherently about demonic hordes of frogs ravaging the world.

Tsathars (1d4+3): HD 2; AC 3[16]; **Atk** weapon (1d8) and bite (1d4); or 2 claws (1d6) and bite (1d4); **Move** 12 (swim 12) or leap (30ft); **Save** 16; **AL** C; **CL/XP** 3/60; **Special:** amphibious, implant (die in 2 weeks, *cure disease* heals), leap (30ft), slimy (difficult to grapple or trap). (see **Appendix A: New Monsters**)
Equipment: Bag containing collection of humanoid finger bones and skeletal toes. One of the tsathars carries a silver earplug worth 50 gp.

Will-o'-the-wisps

Many adventurers have gone to their graves mistaking these dancing balls of malevolent light for natural phenomenon. To perpetrate this ruse, these undead abominations flicker and die out much like flammable swamp gas or bioluminescent insects trying to attract a mate. The monsters alternate between dimming their illumination and turning invisible while they approach living targets. When they shock their victims, the **1d3 will-o'-the-wisps** quickly dart away in an effort to repeat the process. As the lingering essence of restless spirits, the undead creatures speak to the characters, lamenting their deaths in this forsaken place while reassuring the adventurers that they will keep them company when they join the will-o'-wisps in the next life. Despite their proclamations and arrogance, the malevolent beings retreat into the darkness if confronting a superior enemy. They watch and wait for another opportunity to attack the trespassers when they are preoccupied with another foe later in their journey.

Will-o'-the-wisps (1d3): HD 9; AC –8[27]; **Atk** shock (2d6); **Move** 18; **Save** 6; **AL** C; **CL/XP** 10/1400; **Special:** lights (brighten or dim, or form wraith-like form). (*Monstrosities* 512)

Izmalli Swamp Set Encounters

This section describes three set encounters you can intersperse into the adventure to nudge the characters in the right direction during their search for the hidden shrine or to further challenge them along the way to their ultimate destination.

Pain and Gain

The cipatenhuas' newfound devotion to Tsathogga has not gone unnoticed. Six days ago, an **azizou (pain demon)** from the Abyss ventured to the island of Tehuatl to join the crocodilian humanoids in their quest to spread the demon prince's diabolical influence throughout the region. The hideous fiend accompanies a **cipatenhua disciple** on this malevolent journey through the wetlands. The demon uses its innate spellcasting to remain invisible throughout the trip while it visually scouts ahead for fresh souls to corrupt and torment. When the azizou locates a potential target, it non-verbally directs its companion to attack its prospective foes with its spells as it stealthily approaches a lone adversary to single out for an attack. When the characters first set eyes upon the demon, read or paraphrase the following description:

Tufts of coarse black hair grow out of the porous, grayish skin of a halfling-sized humanoid with membranous wings flapping over its slender shoulders. Yellowing fangs fill a canine-shaped snout that protrudes from its jackal-like head with bulbous eyes and serpentine, gray pupils. Its digits end in sharp claws that protrude from its bestial appendages.

The cipatenhua disciple carries the heavy load in this combat as the scheming yet not physically powerful demon flits around in the treetops invisible as it waits for another opportunity to descend from the canopy and unleash its claws and teeth on an unsuspecting foe. Although the fiend desires to kill its quarry, it also seeks to corrupt them if it fails to do so. If combat turns against the pair, the demon coerces the cipatenhua disciple to surrender to the characters and lead them to the shrine where the azizou hopes to tempt them to evil later or murder them if they refuse while the odds are in the demon's favor. In this case, the azizou's cipatenhua guide leads the characters to the pond where the cipatenhuas enter the shrine, though it gives no further assistance or information about what awaits them in the tunnels and chambers ahead.

Azizou (Pain Demon): HD 4; HP 26; AC 1[18]; Atk 2 claws (1d4 + rend), bite (1d6); **Move** 12 (flying 12); **Save** 13; **AL** C; **CL/XP** 7/600; **Special:** +1 or better magic weapons to hit, immune to electricity and poison, magic resistance (10%), rending claws, spell-like abilities, telepathy (100ft). (see **Appendix A: New Monsters**)
Spell-like abilities: 3/day—*ESP, fear, invisibility,* and stinking cloud (20ft radius sphere of nauseating gas, save or sickened and unable to act until out of the cloud for 1d4 rounds).
Equipment: *potion of fire resistance.*

Cipatenhua Disciple of Tsathogga: HD 6; HP 41; AC 7[12] or 2[17] (missile) and 4[15] (melee) from *shield* spell; **Atk** 2 claws (1d4) and bite (1d6) or club (1d6) and bite (1d6); **Move** 12 (swim 12); **Save** 11; **AL** N; **CL/XP** 6/400; **Special:** camouflage (1-in-6 chance to spot), cursed (must remain on wet land or 1d6 damage every 10 minutes), spell-like ability, spells (4/2/2 MU), touch of madness (1/day, save or babble incoherently for 1d6+2 rounds).
Spell-like ability: 1/day—*polymorph self* (into giant frog)
Spells: 1st—*charm person, jinx*[c], *magic missile, shield;* 2nd—*invisibility, phantasmal force;* 3rd—*instill madness*[c], *hold person.*
Equipment: club, hide bag with two human skulls and a tsathar hip bone and 3d6 gp that rattle around with these grisly trophies.
[c] See **Appendix C: New Spells**

ORG

For 17 years, Org the river troll has made his home along the banks of the Elcomatl River, living in a simple lean-to adjacent to a large tree. However, all is not as it appears. The distant town of Hrawrg planted an **ogre mage** into the Izmalli Swamp to act as a spy for the Sepultudre, the septet of leaders who rule that settlement. This ogre mage known as Kerrogg merely plays the part of a river troll to the best of his ability. The solitary, misanthropic giant fervently hates the Aztlis and the other humanoids who inhabit the swamp, yet the outwardly feebleminded operative wisely avoids conflicts with the sentient creatures who cohabitate the region alongside him. He does not actively try to make friends out of the fear that appearing "too welcoming" may blow his cover, but he is also careful to avoid creating enemies as well. It takes considerable effort to crack through his acerbic outer shell, yet some local Aztli girls succeeded at the impossible by tapping into the seemingly oafish Kerrogg's perceived love for dance. Blessed with surprisingly nimble feet and an ear for rhythm, with the proper coaxing the giant sometimes joins the Aztli children for a routine they call "the river dance."

Kerrogg's joviality may feel spontaneous, but the covert agent has an ulterior motive for cultivating a "friendship" with the local Aztli children. The young girls enjoy chatting with the so-called "gentle" giant. They provide him a vital lifeline of information about the neighboring human settlements as well as details they overhear their parents discussing about the other people and creatures who inhabit the swamp. The observant giant also uses his eyes and ears to fill in the gaps, as he freely moves about the swamp with barely a second thought from most creatures, including the cipatenhuas who perceive him to be a harmless simpleton.

Naturally, the adventurers' unexpected appearance piques Kerrogg's interest, prompting him to actively yet discreetly seek them out. Kerrogg keeps his distance during his initial forays with the characters, yet when approached, he dons his typical ornery demeanor and keeps the newcomers at arm's length. Although he can certainly hold his own in a fight, Kerrogg would rather avoid bloodshed and work toward a shared goal of ridding the swamp of Tsathogga's blight. The ogre mage has no love for the Aztlis and their gods, but if given a choice between siding with the humans he knows and the deranged cultists he loathes and secretly fears, the giant reluctantly takes sides with his human adversaries. However, it takes some effort to gain Kerrogg's trust. Like the children, Kerrogg's guests can win his confidence by imitating his river dance.

Alternatively, the adventurers can attempt to logically reason with Kerrogg or bribe the ogre mage into divulging information about the cipatenhuas' shrine and their activities. The giant is receptive to the characters' overtures for assistance. Therefore, it takes only a modest payment to convince him to direct them to the shrine's hidden entrance. The characters can also attempt to ply him by sharing their information about other areas of the Izmalli Swamp, though if he senses the characters are fabricating information, he immediately terminates the conversation and demands they leave at once.

On the other hand, Kerrogg loathes taking orders from humans, especially if the adventurers try to bully him into giving them answers. It takes a herculean effort for Kerrogg to give the characters a second chance. He demands they leave at once, and if they refuse, he gives them a frosty sendoff in the form of a cone of frost cast at them.

Of course, the characters may feel that peacefully interacting at all with an evil ogre mage, regardless of his intentions in this matter, presents an unacceptable alternative, or they may simply see ridding Kerrogg from the swamp as an opportunity to kill two birds with one stone, i.e. eliminating a spy working for a sinister enterprise and looting his treasure. In this case, Kerrogg opts for flight over fight, and uses his abilities to turn invisible and escape the adventurers so he can plot his revenge at a later time. He may attempt to lure characters away from the group one at a time and kill them or change his appearance to infiltrate their ranks when they lower their defenses.

Kerrogg, Ogre Mage: HD 5+4; HP 35; AC 4[15]; **Atk** weapon (1d12); **Move** 12 (fly 18, swim 18); **Save** 12; **AL** C; **CL/XP** 7/600; **Special:** regenerate (1hp/round), spell-like abilities. (***Monstrosities*** 359)
Spell-like Abilities: at will—*darkness 15ft radius, invisibility, polymorph self;* 1/day—*charm person,* cone of frost (60ft range, 20ft diameter blast, 8d6 damage to all, save for half), *sleep.*
Equipment: *gauntlets of swimming and climbing, dust of sneezing and choking,* gold locket on a silver chain (120 gp).

THE CAT IN THE HAG'S HAT

The dank recesses of the Izmalli Swamp offer refuge to some of Tehuatl's most malevolent denizens. Eltezcatl, a wicked **hag nymph**, clearly falls into the preceding category. Eltezcatl and her **hellcat** roam through the swamp from dusk until dawn, and there is a 50% chance of encountering them outdoors between mid-morning and late afternoon. If they are not here, the hag and her companion retreat to her abode, which is described later in this section. While venturing through the wilderness, the sly Eltezcatl dons the appearance of a young, vivacious, beautiful Aztli woman curiously walking across the wetlands with her pet cat who stays close to her side. During these daily jaunts, the seemingly carefree hag seeks young children to abduct and either adopt as her own or devour in one of her sickening stews. Her ideal quarry is a newborn or a pregnant woman, though neither of these individuals ever wanders through the swamp alone. Instead, the gregarious woman strikes up conversations with strangers in a subtle attempt to learn about any potential targets residing in the neighboring villages. She prefers speaking with teenagers and lone travelers rather than engaging groups of adults and especially armed warriors.

When Eltezcatl encounters adversaries who may pose a threat to her, she turns invisible and relies upon her cat companion to lure the characters toward the hag's home where a deadly trap awaits them. Indistinguishable from an ordinary housecat, the feline meows and cries as if it was vainly trying to tell the heroes something of great importance. It supplements these verbal cues by intentionally walking toward Eltezcatl's abode and keeping a sharp eye on the adventurers to make sure they are following. If the characters refuse to follow the clever hellcat or ignore it altogether, the monster telepathically communicates to them that they are in great danger unless they obey the cat's instructions, though the cat makes it appear as if someone else is communicating that message.

The hag's thirst for mayhem is limitless, but her patience is not. Eltezcatl quickly wearies of the cat-and-mouse game, which causes her to drop all pretenses and viciously attack characters who refuse to play along with her and her hellcat. If this occurs, she lashes out with her savage claws while her feline companion uses its death gaze ability against what the monster perceives to be the greatest threat. When combat turns against the pair, they immediately dissolve their partnership and go their separate ways in a mad dash to escape the characters and save their miserable lives. In exchange for mercy, the hag and the hellcat are willing to barter information about the location of the cipatenhuas' shrine should the characters ask about it. While neither can pinpoint the exact spot or means of accessing the presumably subterranean compound, they can narrow it down to a much smaller one-square-mile area near the Elcomatl River. They also speculate that the entrance is submerged beneath a small body of water somewhere in that locale.

However, if the characters follow the hellcat to the hag's home, or alternatively, the characters stumble upon it on their own, they discover the sinister fey dwells in a cramped, universally shunned one-room cabin on the edge of a malodorous pond teeming with mosquitoes, leeches, gnats, and bestial scavengers that coalesce around its stinking waters. The roughly 400-square-foot structure has a barely functional door and is cluttered with junk Eltezcatl accumulated over the years. If the characters venture to her home, read or paraphrase the following description of her ramshackle abode's exterior:

Vines, moss, and other vegetation wind their way up the brick walls of a dilapidated structure with a sloped, slate roof and a swollen wooden door fitted into the building's north side. Weeds, saplings, and shrubs grow unchecked on the grounds amid brooks and streams winding their way across the unkempt property.

A character who approaches the residence notices the pungent scent of burnt tobacco lingering in the air. The door is not locked, but the excessive humidity makes the tight-fitting portal impossible to open without exerting some force. It takes a successful Open Doors check to pull the door open in the absence of any other visible entrances into the cluttered abode. Read or paraphrase the following description to a character who peers into the structure's interior:

Piles of filthy clayware and scraps of rotting food litter a disgusting table surrounded by four chairs. A straw pipe, tobacco scraps, and a ceramic bowl also sit atop the table. Mounds of refuse ranging from heaps of dirt and sand to warped branches to wooden containers of dried leaves cover almost the entirety of the floor, making it impossible to walk across the surface without stepping on an intervening object. A moldy, decomposing fur rests atop a crude bed stuffed against the far corner.

Eltezcatl's willingness to leave her presumably prized junk vulnerable to robbers feels out of character for the covetous hag, and that assumption is entirely correct. While most of these objects are worthless knickknacks she picked up over the years, the notion of someone else stealing a useless item from her rankles her to the core. Her primary guardian, a **wood golem** (see **Appendix A: New Monsters**), disguises itself as the table beneath a badly soiled cloth. If the construct hears a voice unaccompanied by Eltezcatl's shrill words, the golem rises from its hiding spot, which signals an **animated jar** to also spring up from the floor and assault the intruders. The animated jar appears to be an ordinary jar even when examined.

Animated Jar: HD 1; HP 4; AC 5[14]; **Atk** slam (1d4); **Move** 9 (fly 12); **Save** 17; **AL** N; **CL/XP** 1/15; **Special:** none. (*Monstrosities* 13)

Eltezcatl, Hag Nymph: HD 10; HP 68; AC 4[15]; **Atk** 2 claws (1d6); **Move** 12; **Save** 5; **AL** C; **CL/XP** 15/2900; **Special:** magic resistance (25%), enervating gaze, half damage cold and fire, spells (4/4/3/2/2). (see **Appendix A: New Monsters**)
Spells: 1st—*charm person, magic missile* (x2), *shield;* 2nd—

invisibility, mirror image, phantasmal force, web; 3rd—*fly, protection from normal missiles, rope trick;* 4th—*ice storm, plant growth;* 5th—*feeblemind, wall of iron.*
Equipment: potion of extra healing, vial of xochitl (see **Appendix B: New Items and Magic**), gold ring inset with lapis lazuli stones (150 gp).

Hellcat: HD 4; HP 23; AC 6[13]; **Atk** 2 claws (1d6), bite (1d4); **Move** 12 (climbing 12); **Save** 13; **AL** C; **CL/XP** 5/240; **Special:** death gaze (1/day, 30ft radius, save or 2d6 damage, if killed *resurrection* or *wish* to revive), death sense (sense characters with half hit points within 120ft), false appearance (appears to be normal housecat), telepathy (60ft). (see **Appendix A: New Monsters**)

Wood Golem: HD 8; HP 40; AC 7[12]; **Atk** 2 slams (2d8); **Move** 9; **Save** 8; **AL** N; **CL/XP** 10/1400; **Special:** immune to most spells (fire-based or spells affecting plants only), vulnerable to fire (200% damage). (see **Appendix A: New Monsters**)

Treasure: Concealed amid the clutter within the home are a spell scroll (lightning bolt), war paint (purple) (see Appendix B: New Items and Magic), and 2 potions of healing. Finding the Shrine

The encounters in the preceding sections give the characters ample clues and assistance in locating the shrine or at least figuring out its probable location. Of course, the adventurers may also rely upon magic to aid them in their quest to root out the concealed shrine. Nonetheless, the heroes may still struggle to devise a feasible means of finding the entrance to Tsathogga's sanctum. If this is the case, you may have the characters encounter the cipatenhua sentries from the following section and give them an opportunity to question the guards about the shrine or use their tracking skills to follow them back to their lair. If the characters discover where to look for the shrine or determine its precise location, proceed to **Part Two** of the adventure.

PART TWO: THE HIDDEN SHRINE OF TMOCANOTZ

The clever cipatenhuas chose an ideal site to build their profane shrine. Situated roughly one-half mile north of the Elcomatl River, the proximity to the waterway grants them easy access to the river while also keeping them far enough from the riverbank to prevent other humanoids from bumbling into their lair accidentally. Nonetheless, the cipatenhuas maintain a vigilant watch over the surrounding area. If the characters venture within one mile of the cipatenhua stronghold, they have a 30% chance of encountering the sentries, including **3 cipatenhuas** and a **crocodile**. If the cipatenhuas spot the characters first, they attempt to hide and ambush the adventurers when they move past them.

The preceding check is made at 10-minute intervals while the adventurers remain within a half-mile radius of the shrine. The characters cannot encounter more than two groups of sentries regardless of how long they remain in the area. Fearing death more than dishonor, the cipatenhuas never flee or surrender. If captured, they never willingly aid the characters, though they can be magically compelled to divulge logistical details about their lair or they can be forced to do so.

Cipatenhuas (3): HD 3; AC 7[12]; **Atk** 2 claws (1d4) and bite (1d6) or club (1d6) and bite (1d6); **Move** 12 (swim 12); **Save** 14; **AL** N; **CL/XP** 3/60; **Special:** camouflage (1-in-6 chance to spot), cursed (must remain on wet land or 1d6 damage every 10 minutes). (see **Appendix A: New Monsters**)

Crocodile: HD 3; AC 4[15]; **Atk** bite (1d6); **Move** 9 (swim 12); **Save** 14; **AL** N; **CL/XP** 3/60; **Special:** none. (*Monstrosities* 77)

Treasure: The cipatenhuas carry a total of 2d6 blue quartz stones (worth 10 gp each) in addition to their listed weapons and armor. One of them also has a pouch containing 4d6 sp and 3d6 gp in addition to a small bronze idol (worth 25 gp) of a gar-like fish. The object has no religious or cultural significance to the cipatenhua, who simply acquired it from an earlier kill.

If the characters successfully circumvent the stronghold's outer sentries, the guards stationed outside the entrance to the cipatenhua stronghold await

AREA C CIPATENHUA STRONGHOLD
HIDDEN SHRINE OF TMOCANOTZ
Side View
Pond
C2
C1
N
C3
T
C2
C1
C11
C12
C4
C5
C7
C10
T
T
C13
S
C6
C16
C8
C9
C15
C14
1 Square - 5 Feet

them. These **4 cipatenhuas** savagely attack any trespassers who venture close to their lair. If the characters approach this area, read or paraphrase the following description:

Moss clings to the branches of overhanging branches and trees, though some of these greenish-brown filaments fall into a pond of stagnant water surrounded by flowering plants. A wooden trident hangs upside down from a cluster of limbs several feet above the water's surface.

Unlike the sentries, the guards emit ear-piercing shrieks to alert the cipatenhuas in the submerged entrance of their subterranean stronghold along the edge of a mossy fen. Furthermore, they never retreat into their lair, forcing the characters to devise a method of locating the submerged entrance at the western edge of the pond behind them.

Cipatenhuas (4): HD 3; **HP** 21, 19, 18, 13; **AC** 7[12]; **Atk** 2 claws (1d4) and bite (1d6) or club (1d6) and bite (1d6); **Move** 12 (swim 12); **Save** 14; **AL** N; **CL/XP** 3/60; **Special:** camouflage (1-in-6 chance to spot), cursed (must remain on wet land or 1d6 damage every 10 minutes). (see **Appendix A: New Monsters**)
Equipment: 1d3 obsidian stones (10 gp each).

The pond's murky waters conceal the submerged entrance to the cipatenhuas' stronghold, but the surrounding area reveals several important clues. Numerous footprints can be found around the water's edge. The tracks lead into and out of the pond rather than move around its edges. The earth around the pond's edges is soft and spongy, but the ground farther away from the pond is yielding but not soggy. The area is slightly elevated, meaning the pond is not fed by groundwater seeping up to the surface. The pond is a fen fed exclusively by precipitation and runoff from other locations rather than groundwater. A character who puts these pieces together may deduce that the pond opens into a subterranean complex. If the characters reach the preceding epiphany, they are faced with the dilemma of finding the entrance to the tunnel. The small pond encompasses an area measuring only 200 square feet and is a mere four feet deep at its nadir. Although drowning in the shallow water is an unlikely possibility, the murky water obscures all sight, effectively rendering characters blind while underwater. A character who takes the plunge into the water can use his hands to probe around the bottom of the pond. Characters have a 1-in-6 chance to notice that the water current flows from east to west, indicating the presence of a subterranean tunnel. Rangers have a 3-in-6 chance to notice this current.

CIPATENHUA SHRINE FEATURES

Naturally, the cipatenhuas designed their stronghold to accommodate them rather than unwelcome visitors. The humanoids packed damp moss onto the walls and ceilings to limit the amount of water entering the complex. However, unless otherwise stated in an area's description, enough liquid seeps through the imperfect system to soak the earthen floor in roughly 1d2 + 1 feet of standing water, making the entire stronghold difficult terrain, though a creature that can swim can move through the corridors and passages uninhibited. The ceilings are 1d4 + 4 feet in height in each separate chamber and passageway. Creatures too tall to stand upright suffer a −1 to-hit penalty while in the area. Opponents have a +1 to-hit bonus made against creatures too large to move about without crouching or stooping. Furthermore, darkness envelops the entire stronghold unless otherwise mentioned in an area's description.

C1: Submerged Tunnel

Striated layers of decomposing plant matter cover the walls of a spiraling subterranean tunnel presumably winding beneath the pond. Water completely fills the entire passage as it gradually descends into the earth.

The decaying organic matter covering the walls impedes the flow of groundwater into the completely submerged, four-foot-diameter underground pipe that descends at a consistent 30-degree angle until it reaches a depth of 25 feet before the tunnel makes a sharp 10-foot-long U-bend. In total, the tunnel traverses a distance of 105 feet, which presents two problems. While the nimble cipatenhuas can easily hold their breath in an aquatic environment and swim through the tight space, larger humanoids weighed down by armor and bulky equipment fare much worse. Furthermore, the cipatenhuas know the passage's twists and turns by heart; the characters almost certainly have no knowledge of the tunnel's length nor its dimensions.

The murky water completely blinds the characters and forces them to hold their breaths or use magic to navigate the narrow tunnels. While characters might normally be able to use their hands to grope around in the darkness to find their way, in this instance, characters must use their hands to help them crawl along the ground. When a character reaches the U-bend at the end of the tunnel, handholds and footholds along the tunnel walls aid creatures climbing up the vertical shaft opening into Area C2.

C2: Cipatenhua Guard Chamber

The vertical shaft submerged in water culminates in a cramped chamber reeking of decay. The obvious source for the pungent odor is a heap of severed humanoid heads in varying states of decomposition piled against the far wall. Crude, grisly artworks apparently painted onto a material appearing to be vellum hang from the walls. Water slowly seeps through seams in the striated layers of plant material covering the ceiling to create pools and puddles on the soggy, earthen floor.

No respite awaits characters who complete the grueling slog through the watery tunnel, though there are only small pools of standing water covering the floor rather than being mired in difficult terrain. Waiting to unceremoniously greet them are **6 cipatenhuas** who stand at the ready to surprise any intruders who emerge from the tunnel. The clever creatures make a loud commotion that alerts attentive listeners within the complex. However, no reinforcements ever arrive to assist the cipatenhuas at this location. The cipatenhuas never retreat and fight until killed.

The cipatenhuas piled 39 humanoid skulls onto the heap of decapitated heads against the far wall. A character who examines the remains confirms that a sharp instrument severed the heads from the attached vertebrae. In all, there are 29 humans, three orcs, two gnolls, two elves, two dwarves, and one halfling. In each case, it takes one round to thoroughly examine the earthly remains.

The three abstract images painted on the organic medium attached to the walls vaguely depict a grotesque amphibian beast with slimy skin, webbed appendages, and a frog's head. However, the artwork appears crude and of poor quality, making it difficult to decipher its subject. Nonetheless, a character can pick out enough details in the painting to determine that it appears to be a depiction of Tsathogga, though it differs from tsathar portraits of their insane deity. The artworks are painted on human rather than animal flesh.

Cipatenhuas (6): HD 3; HP 23, 21, 18x2, 15, 14; AC 7[12]; **Atk** 2 claws (1d4) and bite (1d6) or club (1d6) and bite (1d6), **Move** 12 (swim 12); **Save** 14; **AL** N; **CL/XP** 3/60; **Special:** camouflage (1-in-6 chance to spot), cursed (must remain on wet land or 1d6 damage every 10 minutes). (see **Appendix A: New Monsters**)
Equipment: pouch containing 1d4 blue quartz stones (10 gp each).

C3: Trapped Passageway

The tunnel sharply turns east and ascends slightly where it continues ahead until it twists north. Small puddles of standing water just a few inches deep cover portions of the soil.

The cipatenhuas never venture down this trapped corridor as they intended it to ensnare trespassers exploring their territory. To further entice intruders into venturing down the hallway, the area is normal terrain, making it easy for characters to walk down the slightly elevated passageway. When the characters reach the dotted line marked as "T", read or paraphrase the following description:

The corridor bends southeast and then sharply turns north where piles of manure and rotting food litter the floor and walls at that spot.

The cipatenhuas deliberately packed excrement and other methane-producing materials at the far end of the bend to build up concentrations of the gas in that bend. To prevent the methane gas from spreading beyond this corridor, the cipatenhuas installed hidden vents in the ceiling that allow the gas to flow out of the complex to the surface. Eight tiny holes are bored into the ceiling and walls from the beginning of the corridor to the "T" location.

Methane Trap

At room temperature, combustible methane gas is colorless and odorless, though the manure emits a foul stench. A pressure plate in the floor at the dotted line marked as "T" creates a spark that ignites the explosive methane.

If the trap is triggered, all creatures within 20 feet of the pressure plate take 6d6 points of fire damage, or half as much with a successful saving throw. If an explosion occurs, the cipatenhuas residing in **Area C4** race to the scene to investigate.

If the pressure plate is disabled, a spark or flame from a different source such as a lit torch or fire-based spell can still detonate the methane gas trap even if the characters disarmed the triggering mechanism. In this case, the blast is centered on the ignition source rather than the pressure plate.

C4: Cipatenhua Living Quarters

Five oval piles of submerged, dark green vegetation lie on the floor, presumably serving as crude beds for the chamber's occupants. Several pieces of a hard, chitinous material are also strewn about the floor.

Only **2 cipatenhuas** currently occupy these living quarters while their colleagues tend to sentry and guard duties. If they hear an explosion in **Area C3**, they rush out to investigate the matter. Otherwise, the pair happily feasts on meat plucked from the exoskeletal chunks taken from a giant crab. They remain engrossed in eating until they notice the characters or until the characters interrupt their meal. They then leap to their feet to attack. The chitinous pieces they are eating are the severed legs of a giant crab. The vegetation used for their beds is seaweed.

Cipatenhuas (2): HD 3; HP 20, 15; AC 7[12]; **Atk** 2 claws (1d4) and bite (1d6) or club (1d6) and bite (1d6); **Move** 12 (swim 12); **Save** 14; **AL** N; **CL/XP** 3/60; **Special:** camouflage (1-in-6 chance to spot), cursed (must remain on wet land or 1d6 damage every 10 minutes). (see **Appendix A: New Monsters**)

Treasure: The cipatenhuas hide their belongings underneath the seaweed. A character who pokes around in each individual seaweed bed finds 1d4 bloodstones (10 gp each).

C5: Cipatenhua Living Quarters

> Five oval piles of dark green vegetation lie on the floor beneath the water's surface, presumably serving as crude beds for the chamber's occupants.

The four cipatenhuas and cipatenhua disciple who reside here are currently on guard and sentry duties, leaving their quarters unoccupied at the moment. Being suspicious of their fellow cipatenhuas, these humanoids left nothing behind for the others to steal. The vegetation serving as their beds is seaweed.

C6: Cipatenhua Living Quarters

> Five oval piles of dark green vegetation lie on the floor, which is only covered by a thin layer of water. These heaps of material presumably serve as crude beds for the chamber's occupants.

This chamber is surprisingly dry compared to most others, with only a thin coating of water covering the floor and is not treated as difficult terrain. The **2 cipatenhuas** and **cipatenhua disciple** who dwell here bide their time toying with **2 poisonous snakes** they recently captured. Before devouring them, the trio cruelly taunts the animals. If the cipatenhuas spot the characters, they refocus their attention on the trespassers in their midst. Otherwise, they continue to torment the snakes until the characters rudely break up their extended play session.

Cipatenhuas (2): HD 3; HP 20, 17; AC 7[12]; **Atk** 2 claws (1d4) and bite (1d6) or club (1d6) and bite (1d6); **Move** 12 (swim 12); **Save** 14; **AL** N; **CL/XP** 3/60; **Special:** camouflage (1-in-6 chance to spot), cursed (must remain on wet land or 1d6 damage every 10 minutes). (see **Appendix A: New Monsters**)

Cipatenhua Disciple of Tsathogga: HD 6; HP 32; AC 7[12] or 2[17] (missile) and 4[15] (melee) from *shield* spell; **Atk** 2 claws (1d4) and bite (1d6) or club (1d6) and bite (1d6); **Move** 12 (swim 12); **Save** 11; **AL** N; **CL/XP** 6/400; **Special:** camouflage (1-in-6 chance to spot), cursed (must remain on wet land or 1d6 damage every 10 minutes), spell-like ability, spells (4/2/2 MU), touch of madness (1/day, save or babble incoherently for 1d6+2 rounds). (see **Appendix A: New Monsters**)
Spell-like ability: 1/day—*polymorph self* (into giant frog)
Spells: 1st—*charm person, jinx^c, magic missile, shield*; 2nd—*invisibility, phantasmal force*; 3rd—*instill madness^c, hold person.*
Equipment: club, hide bag with two human skulls and a tsathar hip bone and 3d6 gp that rattle around with these grisly trophies.
^c See **Appendix C: New Spells**

Poisonous Snakes (2): HD 1d6hp; HP 4, 2; AC 5[14]; **Atk** bite (1hp + poison); **Move** 18; **Save** 18; **AL** N; **CL/XP** 2/30; **Special:** lethal poison (+2 save). (*Monstrosities* 438)

Treasure: The cipatenhuas hide their belongings underneath the seaweed. A character who pokes around in each individual seaweed bed finds 2d6 gp scattered inside it.

C7: Cipatenhua Living Quarters

> Five oval piles of dark green vegetation lie on the floor, presumably serving as crude beds for the chamber's occupants.

The two cipatenhuas and three cipatenhua disciples who normally dwell in these quarters are currently outside the stronghold on a hunting excursion. The occupants took their treasures with them, though one of the cipatenhuas hid a curious item within her bedroll. The vegetation serving as their beds is seaweed.

In their absence, a **demonic mist** now loiters in the currently empty living quarters. During the cipatenhuas' last sacrificial rite, the frog priests overseeing the ceremony tapped into the netherworld's entropic energy, which summoned this abyssal monstrosity to this world. The creature blended its misty form into the seaweed. When the characters enter the room, the demonic mist waits for them to let down their guard before it rises from the muck and blasts the adventurers with a *fear* spell. It then attacks, first using its psychic crush attacks to slaughter its foes. If significantly damaged, the monster passes through the walls and retreats deeper into the complex, moving toward **Area C15** where it alerts the frog prince to the presence of intruders and waits for the characters inside the clam shell in the cipatenhua shrine.

Demonic Mist: HD 5; HP 33; AC 3[16]; **Atk** touch (3d6); **Move** 0 (fly 18); **Save** 12; **AL** C; **CL/XP** 10/1400; **Special:** +1 or better magic weapon to hit, gaseous (creatures save or take 1d6 damage while inside mist), immune to acid and cold, magic resistance (30%), psychic crush (3/day, 40ft range, 2d6 damage and sickened for 1d4+1 rounds [−1 penalty to hit, damage, and saving throws], save avoids), resist fire, spell-like abilities, vulnerable to wind. (see **Appendix A: New Monsters**)
Spell-like abilities: at will—detect magic; 1/day—*confusion, fear.*

Treasure: The seaweed bed in the southwestern portion of the room contains a small bronze sculpture of a jaguar (worth 50 gp) associated with the Aztli god Itztliteotl. The cipatenhua understood the object's religious significance, which prompted her to carefully hide the potentially blasphemous item from her fellow cipatenhuas.

C8: Mess Hall

Light from torches ensconced in the walls illuminates the chamber. Dim light extends roughly 15 feet into the tunnel outside the chamber. The floor is wet but not covered in water.

> Bronze and obsidian cutting implements sit atop two deeply gouged granite slabs covered in blue and yellow liquids. Three emaciated and exhausted humans, two men and a woman, use some of these tools to saw through the rigid exoskeleton of an oversized giant crab draped across one of the slabs. The same yellow liquid pooled on the table also covers the rags clinging to their bodies and their exposed skin. A stone basin filled with water stands on the floor in the near corner.

The unpleasant task of butchering the giant crab on the stone slab falls to the **3 captured Aztlis** armed with itzopillis who toil under the brutal direction of **3 cipatenhuas** and a **cipatenhua disciple.** Although armed with butchering implements, the three abused slaves lack the combat training and physical stamina to fight back against their captors. The cipatenhuas ignore the slaves, redirecting their attention to the intruders. The cipatenhua disciple attempts to tip over the stone basin near the entrance (40% chance). If he accomplishes this task, he releases a **swarm of poisonous snakes** that indiscriminately attacks the nearest creature. Obviously, the cipatenhua disciple makes sure to tip the basin away from him and closer to his enemies, though doing so proves to be an inexact science. After one failed attempt, the cipatenhua disciple abandons the effort and attacks the characters with his repertoire of spells until he exhausts them.

Itzatl and Nectli, Aztli Captives, Male Humans (2): HD 1d6hp; HP 3 each; AC 9[10]; **Atk** itzopilli (1d6); **Move** 12; **Save** 18; **AL** Any; **CL/XP** B/10; **Special:** none. (*Monstrosities* 254)
Equipment: itzopilli (see **Appendix B: New Items and Magic**).

Zyotia, Aztli Captive, Female Human: HD 1d6hp; HP 3; AC 9[10]; **Atk** itzopilli (1d6); **Move** 12; **Save** 18; **AL** Any; **CL/XP** B/10; **Special:** none. (*Monstrosities* 254)
Equipment: itzopilli (see **Appendix B: New Items and Magic**).

Cipatenhuas (3): HD 3; HP 19, 16x2; AC 7[12]; Atk 2 claws (1d4) and bite (1d6) or club (1d6) and bite (1d6); **Move** 12 (swim 12); **Save** 14; AL N; CL/XP 3/60; **Special:** camouflage (1-in-6 chance to spot), cursed (must remain on wet land or 1d6 damage every 10 minutes). (see **Appendix A: New Monsters**)

Cipatenhua Disciple of Tsathogga: HD 6; HP 38; AC 7[12] or 2[17] (missile) and 4[15] (melee) from *shield* spell; Atk 2 claws (1d4) or bite (1d6) or weapon (1d6) and bite (1d6); **Move** 12 (swim 12); **Save** 11; AL N; CL/XP 6/400; **Special:** camouflage (1-in-6 chance to spot), cursed (must remain on wet land or 1d6 damage every 10 minutes), spell-like ability, spells (4/2/2 MU), touch of madness (1/day, save or babble incoherently for 1d6+2 rounds). (see **Appendix A: New Monsters**)
  Spell-like ability: 1/day—*polymorph self* (into giant frog)
  Spells: 1st—*charm person, jinx*[c], *magic missile, shield*; 2nd—*invisibility, phantasmal force*; 3rd—*instill madness*[c], *hold person*.
[c] See **Appendix C: New Spells**

Swarm of Poisonous Snakes: HD 5; HP 31; AC 6[13]; **Atk** swarm (1d6 + poison); **Move** 9; **Save** 12; AL N; CL/XP 8/800; **Special:** lethal poison (+2 save).

The male slaves, Itzatl and Nectli, along with their female counterpart Zyotia, were captured while traveling along a well-worn path with 11 others roughly four months ago. Throughout their captivity, they have been systemically tortured, beaten, and malnourished. Six of the group's traveling companions perished from starvation or mistreatment, while the cipatenhuas presumably sacrificed the other five to their malevolent deity, whom they refer to as the "Ciuatl," which translates as frog. The slaves cannot accurately gauge their captors' numerical strength or provide details about the complex other than the mess hall and their filthy quarters in **Area C9**. However, they know their overseers ultimately answer to a priest or some other religious figure who leads the savage humanoids and may hold additional slaves. In addition, the cipatenhuas keep at least one or two giant crabs in a holding tank somewhere in the subterranean complex.

C9: Slaves' Quarters

A rudimentary latticework carved from wood and reinforced with bronze prevents unfettered entrance into the slaves' quarters. The cipatenhuas bolted the device into the doorjamb from the outside. The apparatus can be disengaged from the door frame with a successful Open Doors check made with thieves' tools or it can be forced open with a successful Open Doors check. Dim light from torches ensconced into the wall extends 15 feet into the outer hallway, bathing the slaves' quarters in normal light. The corridor outside the chamber ascends slightly before opening into this area. The earthen floor in the chamber is wet but not covered with water.

Eight wooden poles affixed to the floor and ceiling support 10 hammocks suspended above the ground. Filthy rags, moldy food, and other sundries are scattered about the floor. The wretched stench of sweat and excrement lingers in the dank air.

These spartan quarters provide sleeping accommodations for 10 individuals, though the three slaves currently occupying **Area C8** are the only individuals living here. The quantity of items and bodily waste littering the ground confirms that more than three people once dwelt in these crowded quarters. Otherwise, a thorough search of the slaves' quarters reveals nothing of significance.

C10: Trapped Corridor

Four passages converge in a sunken, elongated intersection.

This juncture connects the living quarters on the western side of the complex with the religious center and work areas in the eastern section. The water here varies between three and four feet in depth, making it easy for cipatenhuas to swim across the water's surface through the intersection containing pit traps triggered by the creature's weight.

Concealed Pit Trap

The cipatenhuas scattered three pit traps throughout this stretch of the corridor. The five-foot-diameter, 30-foot-deep cylindrical pit traps are neatly concealed beneath dirt and other debris scattered on the floor underneath the water. The hinges supporting the traps give way only when subjected to 125 pounds of direct pressure on the spot, which allows the cipatenhuas to harmlessly swim over them without triggering the traps. Likewise, when they parade a giant crab to the mess hall for butchering, the large crustacean is too big to fall into the round hole bored into the ground. In essence, the cipatenhuas' traps are tailormade to capture humans and other humanoids trespassing into their territory.

If the trap is triggered, the creature who steps on the hinged door must succeed on a saving throw or fall into the pit, taking 3d6 points of damage from the plunge and an additional 1d6 points of damage from shards of obsidian imbedded in the floor. The spring supporting the hinged, watertight door then slams back into place. To make matters worse, the shaft fills with 1d4 feet of water. It takes a successful Open Doors check to reopen the door from inside or outside the pit. Alternatively, placing 125 pounds of direct pressure on the door is sufficient to reopen it as well, though the door springs shut again if the weight is removed and quickly fills with water, which could potentially drown a creature at the bottom of the shaft.

C11: Food Supply

Four sets of brackets affixed to the outer walls of the entrance support long wooden poles that function as makeshift cell bars. The poles comfortably sit inside the brackets, forming a secure pen for the creature trapped inside while allowing someone who can manipulate objects to easily remove the poles.

A rudimentary cell door constructed from bronze brackets and wooden poles prevents unfettered egress from a holding pen.

During their periodic raids, the cipatenhuas capture giant crabs and venomous snakes for later consumption. The humanoids currently keep a **giant crab** captive in this holding tank, which is partially filled with water. The beast attacks any creature foolish enough to enter its domain. If the characters are intent on killing the overgrown crustacean without risking injury to themselves, they can fire ranged weapons between the wooden poles that act as bars. However, in this circumstance, you can opt to award the characters fewer experience points for essentially shooting a fish in a barrel.

Giant Crab: HD 3; HP 21; AC 3[16]; Atk 2 pincers (1d6+2); **Move** 9; **Save** 14; AL N; CL/XP 3/60; **Special:** none. (*Monstrosities* 74)

C12: Armory

Immediately after passing **Area C11**, characters have a 2-in-6 chance to hear the distinct sound of metal striking metal and see dim light originating from the armory. The floor in this area is wet but not submerged beneath water as it is slightly elevated and has drains running along the edge of the floor. If characters spend at least one minute in the hallway observing and listening, they also overhear voices. A character who speaks dwarvish recognizes the language's inflections as dwarvish but cannot discern what is being said amid the cacophony of clanging hammers.

Two sooty male dwarves pound away at a piece of molten metal atop an anvil, while a third member of the team monitors a nearby kiln. Water, presumably from the swamp or pond above the complex, cascades down the walls from cracks in the ceiling and then drains into even wider fissures in the floor along the room's edges. Two bronze battleaxes rest on the floor near the kiln along with metal forceps. Rags heaped along the near wall presumably function as crude bedding for the occupants.

The **3 dwarven metalworkers** tirelessly work under the direction of **2 cipatenhua disciples** and a **cipatenhua frog priest** who intently watch while the dwarven team of Dhumgurin, Erinri, and Vormic Harlbrun feverishly forge his ceremonial bronze dagger. If the characters intrude on the dwarves' efforts, the frog priest emits its crazed croak attack to try to prevent spellcasters from using spells. If the characters surround him or bear down on him too quickly to safely use his spells, he attacks with his bite and greatclub. The deranged frog priest continually babbles throughout the battle and hurls bizarre insults at any Aztli adversaries, especially those who venerate Itztliteotl. He verbally expresses his desire to "feast on their putrid entrails," "clamp his jaws down onto their luscious flesh," and "spill their blood for the Ciuatl's lecherous tongue." He emits an unnerving croaking laugh between these illogical phrases.

Meanwhile, the two cipatenhua disciples unleash their most potent magic at their enemies, blasting characters with their ranged spells before engaging in melee combat. The disciples demand the heroes surrender to Tsathogga and comment that the demon prince would enjoy watching their crispy flesh roasting over an open fire.

The dwarves stand their ground yet make no deliberate attempts to join in the combat. However, if one of them is adjacent to the same foe as a character, the emboldened dwarf takes a swing at his captor. Vormic, the dwarf currently holding the hot molten rod in his forceps, tries to hit one of the cipatenhuas with the searing object, which deals 1d6 points of damage from the strike plus 1d6 points of fire damage.

The cipatenhuas captured the three dwarven cousins approximately three months ago. Although they live in squalor, the malevolent humanoids treat these skilled artisans far better than their menial human laborers. Despite receiving full rations of food, less direct oversight, and avoiding regular abuse at the cipatenhuas' hands, the dwarves long to escape their captivity. However, they have never ventured past **Area C10** and have had contact only with the frog priest and his cipatenhua underlings. However, they believe the frog priest answers to a higher authority within the complex.

The kiln reaches a maximum temperature high enough to forge bronze, but insufficient to smelt iron. The oven contains most of the heat internally, while the chilly water cascading down the walls operates as a natural air conditioning unit.

Cipatenhua Disciples of Tsathogga (2): HD 6; HP 38, 32; AC 7[12] or 2[17] (missile) and 4[15] (melee) from *shield* spell; **Atk** 2 claws (1d4) or bite (1d6) or weapon (1d6) and bite (1d6); **Move** 12 (swim 12); **Save** 11; **AL** N; **CL/XP** 6/400; **Special:** camouflage (1-in-6 chance to spot), cursed (must remain on wet land or 1d6 damage every 10 minutes), spell-like ability, spells (4/2/2 MU), touch of madness (1/day, save or babble incoherently for 1d6+2 rounds). (see **Appendix A: New Monsters**)
Spell-like ability: 1/day—*polymorph self* (into giant frog)
Spells: 1st—*charm person, jinx^c, magic missile, shield*; 2nd—*invisibility, phantasmal force*; 3rd—*instill madness^c, hold person*.
^c See **Appendix C: New Spells**

Cipatenhua Frog Priest of Tsathogga: HD 6; HP 40; AC 7[12]; **Atk** 2 claws (1d4) or bite (1d6) or weapon (1d6) and bite (1d6); **Move** 12 (swim 12); **Save** 11; **AL** C; **CL/XP** 6/400; **Special:** camouflage (1-in-6 chance to spot), crazed croak (1/day, save or lose focus for 1d6+2 rounds), cursed (must remain on wet land or 1d6 damage every 10 minutes), spell-like ability, spells (2/2/1/1 Clr). (see **Appendix A: New Monsters**)
Spell-like ability: 1/day—*polymorph self* (into giant frog).
Spells: 1st—*bloodbath^c, cause light wounds*; 2nd—*hold person, silence 15ft radius*; 3rd—*flay skin^c*; 4th—*cause serious wounds*.
^c See **Appendix C: New Spells**

Dhumgurin, Erinri, and Vormic Harlbrun, Male Dwarves (3): HD 2; HP 14, 12x2; AC 9[10]; **Atk** hammer (1d6); **Move** 9; **Save** 16; **AL** N; **CL/XP** 2/30; **Special:** darkvision (60ft), detect attributes of stonework. (***Monstrosities*** 149)
Equipment: hammer.

C13: Frog Priest Quarters

Unlike the other areas in this complex, the ceiling in this chamber reaches a height of 12 feet, with the hammocks suspended six feet above the ground.

Four wooden poles embedded into the ground support two hammocks stretched across a pool of murky water covering a large portion of the floor. Two conch horns and a closed scallop shell rest on the floor against the near corner.

While one of the complex's two frog priests oversees the dwarves' activities in **Area C12**, the other **cipatenhua frog priest** peacefully sleeps in the hammock suspended over the pool. The seemingly helpless cipatenhua frog priest appears to be at the characters' mercy as he blissfully dreams of wanton slaughter. However, the frog priest is not alone. A **swarm of poisonous frogs** occupies the pool beneath the hammocks, which are intentionally placed three feet above the water. The poisonous frogs do not attack the cipatenhua frog priest. The hungry beasts hide in the cloudy waters of the four-foot-deep pond. The cipatenhua frog priests trained the frogs to remain within the pond to act as a potential food source and as guardians.

Nonetheless, when creatures other than the cipatenhuas come within five feet of the pool's edges, the swarm emerges from the muck to feed if it detects their presence, most likely through its sense of smell if the area remains dark. The mindless frogs cannot discern the cipatenhua frog priest from other creatures, though the swarm generally attacks the first creature it detects, other than the cipatenhuas, and continues to envelop that foe until it slays the hapless victim and moves onto the next closest target. Fully aware of the swarm's tendencies, the frog priest keeps his distance from the frogs whenever possible.

Cipatenhua Frog Priest of Tsathogga: HD 6; HP 37; AC 7[12]; **Atk** 2 claws (1d4) or bite (1d6) or weapon (1d6) and bite (1d6); **Move** 12 (swim 12); **Save** 11; **AL** C; **CL/XP** 6/400; **Special:** camouflage (1-in-6 chance to spot), crazed croak (1/day, save or lose focus for 1d6+2 rounds), cursed (must remain on wet land or 1d6 damage every 10 minutes), spell-like ability, spells (2/2/1/1 Clr). (see **Appendix A: New Monsters**)
Spell-like ability: 1/day—*polymorph self* (into giant frog).
Spells: 1st—*bloodbath^c, cause light wounds*; 2nd—*hold person, silence 15ft radius*; 3rd—*flay skin^c*; 4th—*cause serious wounds*.
^c See **Appendix C: New Spells**

Swarm of Poisonous Frogs: HD 4; HP 27; AC 8[11]; **Atk** swarm (1d6 + poison); **Move** 9 (swim 12); **Save** 13; **AL** N; **CL/XP** 4/120; **Special:** poison (save or die). (see **Appendix A: New Monsters**)

Treasure: The frog priests keep their baubles and curiosities inside the conch horns and oversized scallop shell. One conch horn contains six silver nuggets (worth 10 gp each) and four tin nuggets (worth 1 gp). The second conch horn holds 35 gp and two garnets (worth 100 gp each). It takes a successful Open Doors check to pry open the scallop shell. The characters find seven pearls (worth 100 gp each), an *arrow of flesh finding* (see **Appendix B: New Items and Magic**), and a *potion of growth*.

C14: Mine

Crudely cut passages carved into the earth and stone create a honeycomb of soggy yet not deluged corridors and chambers in a confined area. Loose chunks of rock and soil litter the floor alongside the occasional chisel or pick.

The dwarves toiling in **Area C12** occasionally venture into these twisting, wet mine shafts to extract raw materials from the exposed rock to forge objects in the cipatenhuas' foundry. The metals protruding from the cut surfaces are tin, brass, and iron with small deposits of agate stones. A character who spends an hour chipping away searching for these materials recovers 4d6 gp worth of metal and gems up to a maximum of 40d6 gp of materials yielded for all characters, though the noise may attract the attention of cipatenhuas and

creatures in other areas. The dwarves and cipatenhuas who oversee them keep their distance from the **4 t'shanns** that burrow through the walls and floors blissfully devouring any minerals embedded within the dirt and rocks. The small, slug-like creatures secrete powerful digestive enzymes that dissolve stone and allow them to burrow through these materials.

The t'shanns are not aggressive. They monitor the activities of trespassers from afar if they detect them, though they take no actions to directly avoid them or attack them. However, merely approaching within 30 feet of these strange creatures may remove any self-control the characters may have. The strange thoughts sifting through the t'shanns' brains inadvertently affect the actions of sentient creatures. If the characters intentionally or unintentionally attack the t'shanns, the aberrations fight back to the death.

T'shanns (4): HD 4; **HP** 29, 26, 25, 20; **AC** 9[10]; **Atk** strike (1d4); **Move** 6 (burrow 6); **Save** 13; **AL** N; **CL/XP** 4/120; **Special:** alien thoughts (30ft radius, save or affected by confusion as spell), spew (10ft radius, acid spray, 1d4 damage, save for half). (see **Appendix A: New Monsters**)

C15: Cipatenhua Shrine

The sounds of bizarre chanting and the rancid stench of decay fill the area outside the intersections branching off to **Areas C13** and **C14**. In addition, the passages outside the shrine descend at a decline between 15 and 30 degrees, a characteristic all characters notice.

The brutal cipatenhuas disembowel their victims on the round pedestal and hurl their organs and entrails into the open clam shell where they slowly rot and decay amid their scraped larger bones. The wicked creatures then attach their finger bones to the strands of seaweed hanging from the ceiling. Although the pieces of vegetation affixed to the ceiling are not bunched close enough together to form a contiguous curtain, the strips of solid material are present in sufficient numbers to cause the shrine to be a lightly obscured area.

The **2 cipatenhua disciples** and **Griigg**, the **cipatenhua frog prince** who rules the complex, engage in rhythmic chanting, though they have no victim to sacrifice at the moment. The trio are currently participating in a war chant rather than a religious ritual. The cipatenhua frog prince was in the act of inspiring the cipatenhua disciples to venture back onto the surface to retrieve more victims for their vicious rites when the characters presumably crash their party. If the **demonic mist** from **Area C7** retreated here, it hides within the clam shell frog's gaping maw. The creature emerges after 1d2 rounds of combat and joins the fray alongside Tsathogga's deranged minions. However, if the characters defeat the frog prince, the monster flees again, racing back toward the surface in an effort to flee the shrine altogether and wreak mayhem elsewhere in the swamp.

When the cipatenhuas finally notice the intrusion, the triad springs into action and unleashes a flooded room trap designed to even the odds against their land-based foes. As the water fills the chamber, they leap into the water and attack the characters with their melee weapons. The frog prince loudly boasts of Tsathogga's greatness and curses Itztliteotl as the blasphemous god who condemned his people to the island's dank marshes and swamps. He decries his longing to walk among the grasses and climb the highest peaks yet spends his days in a bleak, subterranean world. Griigg boasts that his offerings of flesh and blood have earned him the Frog God's favor when his demonic servants walk the earth and spread pain and suffering across the land. Despite his physical strength, Griigg has less magical power than his counterparts. He rushes into battle wildly swinging his greatclub at an injured character against whom he is most effective.

The disciples fight as a team, targeting the enemy they deem to be the physically weakest or is obviously the smallest opponent. They begin the onslaught with their spells and then move in for the kill against their designated adversary. The cipatenhua disciples never surrender or retreat with their leader present, though they may attempt to flee if the characters kill the frog prince first. Otherwise, the trio fights to the death.

Cipatenhua Disciples of Tsathogga (2): HD 6; HP 41, 39; AC 7[12] or 2[17] (missile) and 4[15] (melee) from *shield* spell; **Atk** 2 claws (1d4) or bite (1d6) or club (1d6) and bite (1d6); **Move** 12 (swim 12); **Save** 11; **AL** N; **CL/XP** 6/400; **Special:** camouflage (1-in-6 chance to spot), cursed (must remain on wet land or 1d6 damage every 10 minutes), spell-like ability, spells (4/2/2 MU), touch of madness (1/day, save or babble incoherently for 1d6+2 rounds). (see **Appendix A: New Monsters**)
Spell-like ability: 1/day—*polymorph self* (into giant frog)
Spells: 1st—*charm person, jinx*[c], *magic missile, shield*; 2nd—*invisibility, phantasmal force*; 3rd—*instill madness*[c], *hold person*.

Cipatenhua Frog Prince: HD 8; HP 57; AC 6[13]; **Atk** 2 claws (1d4+3) and bite (1d6) or *+1 greatclub* (1d8+4) and bite (1d6); **Move** 12 (swim 12); **Save** 8; **AL** C; **CL/XP** 9/1100; **Special:** camouflage (1-in-6 chance to spot), cursed (must remain on wet land or 1d6 damage every 10 minutes), spell-like ability, Tsathogga's cursed touch (1/day, successful strike, additional 3d6 damage + curse, save or –2 to hit, saves, and damage for 48 hours; if killed, body turns to festering pustules of rancid flesh [*resurrection* or *wish* to restore]). (see **Appendix A: New Monsters**)
Spell-like ability: 1/day—*polymorph self* (into giant frog).
Equipment: *+1 greatclub*, unholy symbol of Tsathogga.

Flooded Chamber Trap

The cipatenhuas deliberately placed their shrine at a lower depth than the remainder of their complex to allow them to rapidly fill the room with water. To activate the trap, one of the cipatenhuas must sharply tug on a strand of tightly wrapped copper cable just above the rounded stone painted to resemble a strand of seaweed. Doing so opens a watertight trapdoor built into the ceiling. When the portal opens, water rapidly pours into the room at a rate of 1d3 feet per round up to a maximum depth of four feet. Creatures submerged beneath the water may eventually drown. The water deals no damage, but on the round when the water first rushes into the room, all characters in the shrine must succeed on a saving throw or be knocked prone. The cipatenhuas use the round stone, which the characters can identify as quartz, to perform their grisly rites. Much like the indigenous Aztlis who perform ritualistic humanoid sacrifices, the cipatenhuas use the flint dagger on the stone to remove their victims' internal organs in an offering to Tsathogga. A living creature who touches or comes into physical contact with the stone takes 1d6 points of damage and is stunned for 1d4 rounds while experiencing a vision of countless hordes of frogs inhabiting a bleak, subterranean cavern stretching for miles in every direction (save avoids damage and stunning). The clam shell adjacent to the stone contains an assortment of skulls, vertebrae, and long bones harvested from dozens of individuals as well as a faux tongue stitched together from excess sinew and muscle repurposed from their victims' bodies. The mollusk carapace measures almost eight feet in length and is four feet wide and four feet high. An adventurer who sifts through the assortment of skeletal remains confirms that the overwhelming majority of the remains are of human origin.

C16: Frog Prince's Quarters

Two wooden poles embedded into the ground support a luxurious hammock. Niches dug into the walls contain an impressive collection of pelvic bones.

In an unusual twist, the cipatenhua frog prince collected his adversaries' pelvic bones as macabre trophies. Most are intact, though some are broken in half or fragmented into smaller pieces. It is impossible to associate the skeletal remains with any specific individuals, though an examination of the 43 pelvises determines that almost all of them are human and roughly half of them are female. The hammock is spun from silk, making it very unusual and rare.

The frog prince conceals his treasure behind one of the niches. Twisting the eastern pole supporting the hammock one full rotation counterclockwise opens the niche.

Treasure: The characters can disentangle the frog prince's silk hammock (worth 50 gp) from its supports. The small niche behind the secret panel holds a leather pouch containing 423 gp and six corals (worth 100 gp each). There is also a *potion of giant strength*, a *cuacalalatli of the beast (frog)* (see **Appendix B: New Items and Magic**) taken from a trespasser, and a *ring of poison resistance*, also removed from the finger of a former adventurer.

Concluding the Adventure

If you used this adventure as a side trek for ***The Re-education of Coyotl***, the characters have rid the Izmalli Swamp of the Tsathogga-worshipping branch of the cipatenhuas who recently migrated to the wetland and may proceed back to Teohuacan to investigate the events at the calmecac. If the characters defeated Griigg and his two frog priests, any remaining cipatenhuas in the region ultimately disperse back to their marsh without their religious leaders. However, unless the characters destroy the altar in **Area C15**, the tsathars locate the hidden shrine in 1d3 weeks and repopulate the unholy site venerating Tsathogga. In a strange twist, Org, the ogre mage masquerading as a river troll, seeks out the adventurers who destroyed Tsathogga's enclave and offers them safe passage to his home settlement in the Tepepan Mountains if the need to visit ever arises. The characters are also free to use this adventure as the launching point for the preceding adventure as one of the freed slaves may ask the characters to escort him or her back home to the neighboring town.

Appendix A: New Monsters

The following monsters are found in this adventure:

Azizou (Pain Demon)

Hit Dice: 4
Armor Class: 1[18]
Attack: 2 claws (1d4), bite (1d6)
Special: +1 or better magic weapons to hit, immune to electricity and poison, magic resistance (10%), rending claws, spell-like abilities, telepathy (100ft).
Move: 12/12 (fly)
Saving Throw: 13
Alignment: Chaos
Number Encountered: 1d4, 2d6
Challenge Level/XP: 7/600

Azizou are relentless combatants that love to inflict pain and suffering on their opponents in combat. Azizoiu have jackal heads, grayish skin covered in patches of course, black hair, and large, round eyes with slit pupils of gray. Membranous wings protrude from their backs and their hands and feet end in talons. A combatant hit by both of an azizou's claw attacks in the same round must succeed on a saving throw or suffer an additional 1d6 points of damage as the demon rends its flesh. Three times per day, azizous can cast *ESP, fear, invisibility*, and create a *stinking cloud within 90 feet. The 20-foot-radius sphere sickens anyone inside the gas who fails a saving throw, leaving them retching while they remain in the gas and for 1d4 + 1 rounds afterward.*

Azizou (Pain Demon): HD 4; **AC** 1[18]; **Atk** 2 claws (1d4 + rend), bite (1d6); **Move** 12 (fly 12); **Save** 13; **AL** C; **CL/XP** 7/600; **Special:** +1 or better magic weapons to hit, immune to electricity and poison, magic resistance (10%), rending claws (if both claws hit target, save or additional 1d6 damage), spell-like abilities, telepathy (100ft).
Spell-like abilities: 3/day—*ESP, fear, invisibility*, and stinking cloud (20ft radius sphere of nauseating gas, save or sickened and unable to act until out of the cloud for 1d4 rounds).

Cipatenhua

Hit Dice: 3
Armor Class: 7[12]
Attack: 2 claws (1d4) and bite (1d6) or weapon (1d6) and bite (1d6)
Special: Camouflage, cursed
Move: 12/12 (swim)
Saving Throw: 14
Alignment: Chaos
Number Encountered: 1d4, 2d4
Challenge Level/XP: 3/60

The reptilian cipatenhuas resemble humanoid crocodiles. They attack with their claws and bite, but also wield weapons against their foes. They often hide in the waterways and strike fast from camouflage (1-in-6 chance to spot). The cipatenhuas are cursed and must always remain in contact with water, wet earth, or another wet surface. If they are not, they take 1d6 points of damage every 10 minutes.

Cipatenhua: HD 3; **AC** 7[12]; **Atk** 2 claws (1d4) and bite (1d6) or weapon (1d6) and bite (1d6); **Move** 12 (swim 12); **Save** 14; **AL** Chaos; **CL/XP** 3/60; **Special:** camouflage (1-in-6 chance to spot), cursed (must remain on wet land or 1d6 damage every 10 minutes).

Cipatenhua Disciple of Tsathogga

Hit Dice: 6
Armor Class: 7[12]
Attack: 2 claws (1d4) and bite (1d6) or weapon (1d6) and bite (1d6)
Special: Camouflage, cursed, spell-like ability, spells
Move: 12/12 (swim)
Saving Throw: 11
Alignment: Chaos
Number Encountered: 1d2
Challenge Level/XP: 6/400

The cipatenhua disciple of Tsathogga is a humanoid crocodile spellcaster of the Frog God. They attack with their claws and bite, but also wield weapons against their foes. They often hide in the waterways and strike fast from camouflage (1-in-6 chance to spot). The cipatenhuas are cursed and must always remain in contact with water, wet earth, or another wet surface. If they are not, they take 1d6 points of damage every 10 minutes. Once per day, the disciple can touch an opponent and cause them to babble incoherently for 1d6 + 2 rounds if they fail a saving throw. They can also polymorph themselves into a giant frog once per day. The disciple is a 6th-level magic-user.

Cipatenhua Disciple of Tsathogga: HD 6; **AC** 7[12] or 2[17] (missile) and 4[15] (melee) from *shield* spell; **Atk** 2 claws (1d4) and bite (1d6) or weapon (1d6) and bite (1d6); **Move** 12 (swim 12); **Save** 11; **AL** C; **CL/XP** 6/400; **Special:** camouflage (1-in-6 chance to spot), cursed (must remain on wet land or 1d6 damage every 10 minutes), spell-like ability, spells (4/2/2 MU), touch of madness (1/day, save or babble incoherently for 1d6+2 rounds).
Spell-like ability: 1/day—*polymorph self* (into giant frog)
Spells: 1st—*charm person, jinx*[c], *magic missile, shield*; 2nd—*invisibility, phantasmal force*; 3rd—*instill madness*[c], *hold person*.
[c] See **Appendix C: New Spells**

Cipatenhua Frog Priest

Hit Dice: 6
Armor Class: 7[12]
Attack: 2 claws (1d4) and bite (1d6) or club (1d6) and bite (1d6)
Special: Camouflage, crazed croak, cursed, spell-like ability, spells
Move: 12/12 (swim)
Saving Throw: 11
Alignment: Chaos
Number Encountered: 1d2
Challenge Level/XP: 6/400

The cipatenhua frog priest of Tsathogga is a humanoid crocodile divine spellcaster of the Frog God. They attack with their claws and bite, but also wield weapons against their foes. They often hide in the waterways and strike fast from camouflage (1-in-6 chance to spot). The cipatenhuas are cursed and must always remain in contact with water, wet earth, or another wet surface. If they are not, they take 1d6 points of damage every 10 minutes. Once per day, the frog priest can issue a crazed croak that causes anyone within 30 feet who fails a saving throw to be disturbed by horrific visions and unable to concentrate on a specific task (fighting, spellcasting, etc.) for 1d6 + 2 rounds. They can also polymorph themselves into a giant frog once per day. The frog priest is a 6th-level cleric.

Cipatenhua Frog Priest of Tsathogga: HD 6; **AC** 7[12]; **Atk** 2 claws (1d4) and bite (1d6) or club (1d6) and bite (1d6); **Move** 12 (swim 12); **Save** 11; **AL** C; **CL/XP** 6/400; **Special:** camouflage (1-in-6 chance to spot), crazed croak (1/day, save or lose focus for 1d6+2 rounds), cursed (must remain on wet land or 1d6 damage every 10 minutes), spell-like ability, spells (2/2/1/1 Clr).
Spell-like ability: 1/day—*polymorph self* (into giant frog).
Spells: 1st—*bloodbath*[c], *cause light wounds*; 2nd—*hold person, silence 15ft radius*; 3rd—*flay skin*[c]; 4th—*cause serious wounds*.
[c] See **Appendix C: New Spells**

Cipatenhua Frog Prince

Hit Dice: 8
Armor Class: 6[13]
Attack: 2 claws (1d4+3) and bite (1d6) or greatclub (1d8+3) and bite (1d6)
Special: Camouflage, cursed, immune to charm and fear, spell-like

ability, Tsathogga's cursed touch
Move: 12/12 (swim)
Saving Throw: 8
Alignment: Chaos
Number Encountered: 1
Challenge Level/XP: 9/1,100

The cipatenhua frog prince is a humanoid crocodile. It attacks with its claws and bite, but also wields a greatclub. It often hides in the waterways and strikes fast from camouflage (1-in-6 chance to spot). Cipatenhuas are cursed and must always remain in contact with water, wet earth, or another wet surface. If they are not, they take 1d6 points of damage every 10 minutes. Once per day, the frog prince can target one creature with an attack that does an additional 3d6 points of damage and curses the target if it fails a saving throw. On a failure, the creature suffers a –2 penalty to hit, saves, and damage for 48 hours (or until a *remove curse* spell is cast on the creature). If a creature dies from this attack, its body turns to festering pustules of rancid flesh (*resurrection* or *wish* to restore). The frog prince can polymorph itself into a giant frog once per day.

Cipatenhua Frog Prince: HD 8; AC 6[13]; Atk 2 claws (1d4+3) and bite (1d6) or greatclub (1d8+3) and bite (1d6); **Move** 12 (swim 12); **Save** 8; AL C; CL/XP 9/1100; **Special:** camouflage (1-in-6 chance to spot), cursed (must remain on wet land or 1d6 damage every 10 minutes), spell-like ability, Tsathogga's cursed touch (1/day, successful strike, additional 3d6 damage + curse, save or –2 to hit, saves, and damage for 48 hours; if killed, body turns to festering pustules of rancid flesh [*resurrection* or *wish* to restore]).
Spell-like ability: 1/day—*polymorph self* (into giant frog).

DEMONIC MIST

Hit Dice: 5
Armor Class: 3[16]
Attack: touch (3d6)
Saving Throw: 12
Special: +1 or better weapon to hit, gaseous, immune to acid and cold, magic resistance (30%), psychic crush, resist fire, spell-like abilities, vulnerable to wind
Move: 0 (fly 18)
Alignment: Chaos
Number Encountered: 1d2 or 1d4+2
Challenge Level/XP: 10/1,400

Indigenous to the planes of Chaos, demonic mists occasionally make their way into the world through unholy rites performed by insane clerics or magic-users seeking forbidden lore. Oddly, on this plane, demonic mists are drawn to and most often encountered in areas of consecrated ground, such as graveyards, temples, and holy sites. Demonic mists have voracious appetites and always seem to be on the hunt. They are carnivorous creatures devouring just about anything they came across. Once a demonic mist slays its prey, it moves over the body and rapidly digests it, draining blood and body fluids, and leaving nothing more than a dried husk.

A demonic mist's semi-solid body is composed of a strange, sickly green and ever-shifting mist. It can change its color to a semi-translucent whitish smoke, thereby blending in and hiding in areas of normal fog and mist. When hiding in this way, a demonic mist seeks to quickly close ground with its target and attack from ambush, unleashing its psychic crush at the closest and strongest opponents. Because it is gaseous, a demonic mist can pass through small holes, even cracks, without reducing its speed. It cannot enter water or other liquid. It cannot manipulate objects, and it is vulnerable to wind. Creatures inside the mist must make a saving throw or suffer 1d6 points of damage; the demonic mist heals a like amount of damage.

Three times per day, a demonic mist can attempt to crush the mind of a single creature within 40 feet. The target takes 2d6 points of damage (save avoids) and becomes sickened for 1d4 + 1 rounds, suffering a –1 penalty to hit, damage, and saving throws. A demonic mist can use the following magical abilities: at will—*detect magic*; 1/day—*confusion*, *fear*.

Demonic Mist: HD 5; AC 3[16]; Atk touch (3d6); **Move** 0 (fly 18); **Save** 12; AL C; CL/XP 10/1400; **Special:** +1 or better magic weapon to hit, gaseous (creatures save or take 1d6 damage while inside mist), immune to acid and cold, magic resistance (30%), psychic crush (3/day, 40ft range, 2d6 damage and sickened for 1d4+1 rounds [–1 penalty to hit, damage, and saving throws], save avoids), resist

fire, spell-like abilities, vulnerable to wind.
Spell-like abilities: at will—*detect magic*; 1/day—*confusion*, *fear*.

GOLEM, WOOD

Hit Dice: 8 (40 hit points)
Armor Class: 7[12]
Attack: 2 slams (2d8)
Saving Throw: 8
Special: +1 or better magic weapons to hit, immune to most spells, vulnerable to fire
Move: 9
Alignment: Neutrality
Number Encountered: 1 or 3
Challenge Level/XP: 10/1,400

Arcane spellcasters used several ancient texts to arrive at a process to create inexpensive yet still quite powerful golems. They had master craftsmen create wood statues with articulating limbs and then performed the proper spells to animate and control them. The statues vary in shape and form and usually have weapons of some sort held in each hand. The wood golems were designed to act as an alarm and a protection against intruders. The golem can often contort itself into another wooden form (such as a rough approximation of a table or other large piece of furniture).

Wood golems are affected only by fire-based spells or spells that affect plants such as *hold plant* or *warp wood* (which does 3d6 points of damage, no save). *Repel wood* holds the wood golem at bay, but doesn't harm it.

Wood Golem: HD 8; HP 40; AC 7[12]; Atk 2 slams (2d8); **Move** 9; **Save** 8; AL N; CL/XP 10/1400; **Special:** immune to most spells (fire-based or spells affecting plants only), vulnerable to fire (200% damage).

HAG NYMPH

Hit Dice: 10
Armor Class: 4[15]
Attack: 2 claws (1d6)
Saving Throw: 5
Special: enervating gaze, magic resistance (25%), resists cold and fire, spell-like abilities, spells
Move: 12
Alignment: Chaos
Number Encountered: 1 or 3
Challenge Level/XP: 15/2,900

Hag nymphs are hideous, bent crones; their frames are emaciated and almost corpse-like in appearance. They have sickly green skin, thin dark hair and hands that end in wicked claws with filthy nails. Their clothes usually carry the bloodstains of previous victims. Hag nymphs live deep within dark forests in huts composed of mud and timber. These huts are usually well-constructed and littered with the rotting remains of creatures the hag has devoured.

A hag nymph's profane beauty affects all humanoids within 30 feet. Those who look directly at a hag nymph must succeed on a saving throw or be weakened, losing 2d4 points of strength for 1d6 days. Hag nymphs can cast the following spells: Constant—*detect good, detect magic*; At will—*cause light wounds*; 3/day—*cause serious wounds*; 1/day—*polymorph other*. A hag nymph also casts spells as a 10th-level Magic-User (4/4/3/2/2), and a sample spell list is provided below. Hag nymphs take only half normal damage from cold and fire.

Hag Nymph: HD 10; AC 4[15]; Atk 2 claws (1d6); **Move** 12; **Save** 5; AL C; CL/XP 15/2900; **Special:** magic resistance (25%), enervating gaze (save or weakened, lose 2d4 strength for 1d6 days), resist cold and fire (50% damage), spell-like abilities, spells (4/4/3/2/2).
Spell-like abilities: constant—*detect good, detect magic*; at will—*cause light wounds*; 3/day—*cause serious wounds*; 1/day—*polymorph other*.
Spells: 1st—*charm person, magic missile* (x2), *shield*; 2nd—*invisibility, mirror image, phantasmal force, web*; 3rd—*fly, protection from normal missiles, rope trick*; 4th—*ice storm, plant growth*; 5th—*feeblemind, wall of iron*.

Hellcat

Hit Dice: 4
Armor Class: 6[13]
Attack: 2 claws (1d6), bite (1d4)
Saving Throw: 13
Special: Death gaze, death sense, false appearance, telepathy (60ft)
Move: 12/12 (climb)
Alignment: Chaos
Number Encountered: 1, 1d4, 2d4
Challenge Level/XP: 5/240

The hellcat appears, at first glance, as a common housecat, but this is belied by the feline's evil red gaze. The hellcat feeds off souls, often hunting in the night for the weakest humanoids, those lost or nearest death. The hellcat can smell those near death (below half their hit points) within 120 feet. Once located, the hellcat uses its death gaze to steal the creature's soul just before death. It then stealthily flees, if possible, running into the dark as quickly as it can after tasting of the dead.

Until the hellcat uses its death gaze, it appears to be nothing more than a normal housecat (although spells and magic items that can see through illusions show its true nature). Once per day, a hellcat can target its death gaze on one creature within 30 feet, which must make a saving throw or take 2d6 points of damage. If the creature dies from this damage, it can be restored to life only by using a *resurrection* or *wish* spell.

Hellcat: HD 4; **AC** 6[13]; **Atk** 2 claws (1d6), bite (1d4); **Move** 12 (climb 12); **Save** 13; **AL** C; **CL/XP** 5/240; **Special:** death gaze (1/day, 30ft radius, save or 2d6 damage, if killed *resurrection* or *wish* to revive), death sense (sense characters with half hit points within 120ft), false appearance (appears to be normal housecat), telepathy (60ft).

Ooze, Mudbog

Hit Dice: 6
Armor Class: 8[11]
Attack: slam (2d6)
Special: Acid, camouflage, engulf, immune to blunt weapons
Move: 6/9 (swim)
Saving Throw: 11
Alignment: Neutrality
Number Encountered: 1, 1d4
Challenge Level/XP: 6/400

A mudbog ooze appears indistinguishable from a large muddy puddle. It attacks by slamming its opponent with a pseudopod. If the mudbog ooze strikes a foe, it can decide on its next attack to instead engulf that opponent (save avoids). Engulfed opponents take 1d6 points of damage per round from the acidic nature of the ooze. The acid dissolves organic material, but not metal or stone. Any non-magical wooden weapons used to attack a mudbog ooze must make a saving throw or dissolve.

Mudbog Ooze: HD 6; **AC** 8[11]; **Atk** slam (2d6); **Move** 6 (swim 9); **Save** 11; **AL** N; **CL/XP** 6/400; **Special:** acid (dissolves organic material), camouflage (1-in-6 chance to spot), engulf (after strike, can engulf with next successful strike, 1d6 damage per round, save avoids), immune to blunt weapons.

Sloth Viper

Hit Dice: 5
Armor Class: 6[13]
Attack: bite (1d4 + poison)
Special: Poison
Move: 12/12/12 (climb/swim)
Saving Throw: 12
Alignment: Neutrality
Number Encountered: 1, 1d4
Challenge Level/XP: 6/400

Sloth vipers are emerald-colored snakes with bands of gold and black ringing their body. Their tails are tipped with black and their eyes are amber or brown in color. The typical sloth viper is nine to 10 feet long, though they can grow to a length of 20 or more feet. A sloth viper's bite delivers a deadly poison.

Sloth Viper: HD 5; **AC** 6[13]; **Atk** bite (1d4 + poison); **Move** 12 (climb 12, swim 12); **Save** 12; **AL** N; **CL/XP** 6/400; **Special:** poison (save or die).

Swarm of Poisonous Frogs

Hit Dice: 4
Armor Class: 8[11]
Attacks: Swarm (1d6 + poison)
Saving Throw: 13
Special: Poison
Move: 9/12 (swim)
Alignment: Neutrality
Challenge Level/XP: 4/120

Poisonous frog swarms are composed of small, fierce, poisonous frogs. A single poisonous frog is a small dark green frog with black bands or stripes on its hind legs. These stripes function as a warning to predators that the frog is poisonous. The skin of a poisonous frog is very smooth to the touch. The middle digit on each of its extremities is slightly shorter than the others. A poisonous frog swarm delivers its poison with a successful swarm attack.

Swarm of Poisonous Frogs: HD 4; **AC** 8[11]; **Atk** swarm (1d6 + poison); **Move** 9 (swim 12); **Save** 13; **AL** N; **CL/XP** 4/120; **Special:** poison (save or die).

T'shann

Hit Dice: 4
Armor Class: 9[10]
Attacks: strike (1d4)
Saving Throw: 13
Special: Alien thoughts, spew
Move: 6/6 (burrow)
Alignment: Neutrality
Challenge Level/XP: 4/120

The slug-like t'shann has a cylindrical body and a mass of dripping, writhing tentacles at its head. It is brownish gray, with patches of green and black blotches scattered unevenly over its body. Its underside is pasty off-white in color and ripples with the muscular contractions that move the creature along. T'shanns burrow through earth and stone to consume the minerals trapped in the rock. They range anywhere from two to four feet long.

The alien brainwaves of a t'shann have a bizarre effect on intelligent creatures. All living creatures within 30 feet of a t'shann must save or be affected as if by a *confusion* spell. If creatures approach within 10 feet, they must succeed on another save or suffer 1d4 points of damage every round that they remain within 10 feet of the t'shann.

A t'shann can emit a spray of powerful acids from nearly every pore on its body, affecting every creature within 10 feet. This acidic spray does 1d4 points of acid damage (save for half damage).

T'shann: HD 4; **AC** 9[10]; **Atk** strike (1d4); **Move** 6 (burrow 6); **Save** 13; **AL** N; **CL/XP** 4/120; **Special:** alien thoughts (30ft radius, save or affected by confusion as spell), spew (10ft radius, acid spray, 1d4 damage, save for half).

Tsathar (Common)

Hit Dice: 2
Armor Class: 3[16]
Attack: Weapon (1d8) and bite (1d4) or 2 claws (1d6) and bite (1d4)
Saving Throw: 16
Special: Amphibious, implant, leap, slimy
Move: 12/12 (swim)
Alignment: Chaos
CL/XP: 3/60

A tsathar (pronounced "suh-Thar") resembles an upright, humanoid frog with gray flesh and reddish-gold eyes. Its humanoid arms end in wicked claws. Tsathar have little contact with surface-dwelling races, preferring to make their lairs deep underground or in dark swamps. When they lair above ground, they are nocturnal.

A typical tsathar stands six feet tall and weighs about 300 pounds. Tsathar speak their own strange, guttural language and the eldritch speech of demons. Tsathar prefer to use short, barbed spears and curved daggers in combat. They sometimes employ nets as well. They charge into combat with maniacal fury, and rarely use elaborate tactics. They favor leather armor crafted from the hides of the frogs they breed.

Tsathar can leap up to 30 feet horizontally (10 feet vertically) and make an attack in the same round. Tsathar wearing armor heavier than ring armor cannot use this ability.

Tsathar are sexless and reproduce by injecting eggs into living hosts. An egg can be implanted only into an unconscious or restrained host. Giant frogs, which are bred for this very purpose, are the most common host. Accompanying the egg is an anaesthetizing poison that causes the host to fall unconscious for the two-week gestation period of the egg unless the host succeeds on a saving throw. If the save succeeds, the host remains conscious, but is violently ill (–10 penalty to hit and saving throws) 24 hours before the eggs hatch. When the eggs mature, the young tsathar emerge from the host, killing it in the process. A *cure disease* spell rids the victim of the eggs.

Abrupt exposure to bright light (such as sunlight or a *light* spell) blinds tsathars for one round.

Because tsathar continuously cover themselves with muck and slime, they are difficult to grapple. Webs, magic or otherwise, do not affect tsathar, and they usually can wriggle free from most other forms of confinement.

Tsathar (Common): HD 2; **AC** 3[16]; **Atk** weapon (1d8) and bite (1d4); or 2 claws (1d6) and bite (1d4); **Move** 12 (swim 12) or leap (30ft); **Save** 16; **AL** C; **CL/XP** 3/60; **Special:** amphibious, implant (die in 2 weeks, *cure disease* heals), leap (30ft), slimy (difficult to grapple or trap).

APPENDIX B: NEW ITEMS AND MAGIC

The following items and magic are found in this adventure:

NEW ARMOR

Cipacahuipilli. This armor is thin with flat pieces of hide and bone strategically sewn into the fabric to adequately compensate for its lesser thickness. The armor's name comes from the flat sections of crocodile vertebrae and hide stitched into the material at vulnerable spots to improve toughness without adding tremendous weight and bulkiness. Most importantly, the armor's lack of metallic pieces or parts makes it immune to rust and suitable for druids.

TEHUATL ARMOR

Armor Type	Effect on AC from base 9[10]	Weight[1] (pounds)	Cost
	Medium Armor		
Cipacahuipilli	−3[+3]	15	75 gp

[1] Magical armor weighs half normal

NEW WEAPONS

Macuahuitl. Made from hardwood such as oak, this weapon resembles a long, flat paddle with obsidian or flint chips embedded into the weapon's edges. The insertion of these incredibly sharp stones gives the weapon unmatched cutting power at the cost of increased fragility. When you attack a creature with this weapon and roll a 19 or 20 on the attack roll, the weapon deals double damage. Furthermore, the creature struck loses 1d4 hit points each round due to the blade gouging a deep laceration through its flesh. The damage increases by 1d6 if you inflict another deep laceration during a subsequent attack.

However, when you attack a creature with this weapon and roll a 1, you damage the weapon. Your attacks with the weapon suffer a −1 to-hit penalty, and you can no longer inflict a deep laceration. If you damage an already damaged weapon, the weapon breaks, rendering it useless.

TEHUATL WEAPONS

Weapon	Damage	Weight (pounds)	Cost
	Melee Weapon		
Macuahuitl	1d8[1]	2	10 gp

[1] Deals double damage on roll of 19–20; deep cut does 1d4 additional damage per round; second deep cut raises continual damage to 1d6; roll of 1 damages weapon and imposes −1 to-hit penalty; second roll of 1 destroys weapon

NEW EQUIPMENT

Xochitl. A creature that drinks this vial of vanilla-flavored liquid suffers a −1 penalty on saving throws against being put to sleep by magic for one hour. Alternatively, a creature that drinks xochitl less than one hour before resting falls into a deep slumber. A creature who normally needs eight hours of sleep awakens refreshed after four hours of sleep.

MAGIC WEAPONS

ARROW OF FLESH FINDING

This arrow is a *+1 arrow* with the unusual ability to avoid striking inanimate objects in its path. When a character makes a ranged attack roll with the arrow, the target does not gain any AC bonus from being behind cover. If the target's body is made of flesh, the arrow deals 2d6 points of damage on a successful hit. Once an *arrow of flesh finding* hits a target, it becomes a nonmagical arrow.

MISC. MAGICAL ITEMS, GREATER

CUACALALATLI OF THE BEAST

These wooden helmets are shaped into the likenesses of various beast heads. The protective device fits over the head and covers the top and back of the skull as well as the jawline. Anyone wearing one of these helmets gains the animal's abilities. The type of beast associated with the helmet determines its specific properties:

Crocodile: The wearer can slam its target for 1d6 points of damage.

Eagle: The wearer cannot be surprised.

Frog: The wearer can hold his or her breath for 15 minutes and gains a +1 to-hit bonus when fighting underwater.

Jaguar: The wearer gains a +1 bonus to attacks and damage against injured foe.

Monkey: The wearer can scale vertical walls (Climb 9).

Serpent: The wearer can slide through gaps half his or her size.

Usable by fighters and thieves.

WAR PAINT

Typically stored in clay jars, each container holds 1d3 applications of viscous pigments made from dyes and other colorful components. A creature can wear no more than three different colors of paint at a time, and only one color of war paint can be applied to a weapon. Any attempt to apply more colors fails. Each application of paint lasts for one turn regardless of color. The *war paint's* color determines its effects:

Black: The wearer is infused with a dark energy that deals 1d6 points of damage to any creature touched or struck.

Blue: A frigid chill courses through the wearer's body and causes frost to form on any weapon. The cold is harmless to the wearer and the weapon. This cold deals an additional 1d6 points of damage with a successful strike.

Green: The wearer cannot be restrained or paralyzed.

Orange: The wearer is immune to fear.

Purple: The wearer gains a +1 to-hit bonus during combat.

Red: Warmth radiates through the wearer's skin and causes one weapon to glow red-hot. The heat is harmless to the wearer and the weapon. This fiery weapon deals an additional 1d6 points of fire damage.

White: The wearer's weapon deals an additional 1d6 points of damage to undead and fiends.

Yellow: Energy surges within the wearer's body and causes one weapon to crackle with electrical energy. The electricity is harmless to the wearer and the weapon. The weapon deals an additional 1d6 points of electrical damage.

Usable by all classes.

Appendix C: New Spells

The following spells are found in this adventure:

Bloodbath

Spell Level: Cleric, 1st Level
Range: 30 feet
Duration: Immediate

This spell creates 10 gallons of blood within range in an open container. Alternatively, the blood splashes onto all creatures and objects in a 30-foot cube within range. The blood extinguishes exposed flames in the area and is identical in composition to your own blood. Each creature within the area must succeed on a saving throw or drop whatever it is holding and be disgusted for 1 hour. The disgusted creature cannot willingly move closer to the caster and averts its eyes, so as not to see the spellcaster. Creatures that cannot be frightened are still doused in blood but are otherwise not affected by this spell.

Flay Skin

Spell Level: Cleric, 3rd Level; Magic-User, 3rd Level
Range: 30 feet
Duration: Immediate

This spell targets a living creature who takes 1d6 points of damage per level of the caster as portions of its skin are flayed from its body. The creature takes half damage on a successful saving throw and its skin is not flayed. Creatures with flayed skin suffer a +2 penalty to armor class until they receive magical healing.

Instill Madness

Spell Level: Magic-User, 3rd Level
Range: 120 feet
Duration: 1 hour

This spell targets one creature within range who must make a saving throw or succumb to madness for the duration of the spell. The target can decide to move or attack, but when it does, it acts randomly. If it moves, roll a d8 and assign a direction to each die face. It moves in that direction to the extent of its movement. If it attacks, it attacks a random creature within its reach.

Jinx

Spell Level: Magic-User, 1st Level
Range: 30 feet
Duration: Immediate

A creature within range of this spell receives an ominous feeling that something bad is about to happen. If the creature fails a saving throw, it takes a −1 penalty on to-hit rolls, damage, and saving throws for the next hour. A target can be affected by only one *jinx* spell at a time.

The caster can target additional creatures at higher levels: two creatures at 3th level, three creatures at 5th level, and four creatures at 7th level.